Lake's Legacy

K.L. Barstow

To Shadow and Luna
Gone too soon
Never to be forgotten
You left your footprints on my heart

Author's Note

Each book covers the developing relationship between its protagonists. Each book has a HEA, but the ending of each book has a lead-in for the next book.

These books contain sex and violence, along with elements of domestic discipline and BDSM. The stories may also contain triggers. If you don't like stories with these elements, please don't read.

Recommended Reading Order:

Coming Soon

Chapter One: Lake

"You okay there, Lake?" Pirate asks with a laugh.

"Fuck off," I growl, gripping the handrest tighter.

"Why did you agree to go to Ireland with Dixie if you don't like flying," Pirate continues. "Or did you think we were driving there?"

"Seriously, shut up," I growl back.

He's silent for several minutes, but I can feel him looking at me.

"Have you spoken with Olivia recently?" He asks me, and I realize he's trying to distract me from my fear of flying. I should be grateful, but what I want to do is strangle him.

However, I open one eye and glare at him. "I spoke to her after we landed in Ireland and then again just before we left for home. Why?"

"Did she tell you about looking at the photos of the dead women?"

I open the other eye as I nod. My thoughts on Olivia's breakdown after she insisted on looking at the photos of each woman we found in the office building Cleo owns. "Yeah, tore her up."

"Brave woman," Pirate says.

"Have you found anything on her missing friends?"

"No. The police have made no progress. However, they discovered someone tampered with Talia's car. The car broke down a few miles from the hospital. They're still trying to figure out how and when someone sabotaged it."

"Do they think that's how whoever kidnapped her got to her?"

"It's their current theory. They can't find the doctor's car, so there is no way to verify if this is a possible M.O."

"Have they checked the security feed?"

"They have, but the camera angle only covered the car's trunk. No way to see if anyone approached the vehicle from the front."

"Maybe they'll find something," I muse. I know Olivia's concerns for her former coworkers grow stronger every day. Now that we're heading back to New Orleans, Pirate should have more time to help locate them. "Any ideas on how to look for them?"

"I spoke with Dante, and he's permitted me to contact Maestro for help. I want him to run his program against the traffic cam footage for the nights the two women disappeared," Pirate says, nodding toward Dante, sitting with Dixie and Hex.

Dante is the President of the Original Chapter of the Demon Dawgs. It's his mother's plane that we're flying on today. Rather than letting myself remember that we're flying, I watch Dixie take a small box out of his pocket and look at it before returning it. The box contains his mother's engagement and wedding rings. He can't stop himself from checking on them every few minutes after he retrieved them from the safe deposit box.

"Ten bucks says he drops to his knee the second he sees Delphine," Pirate says with a smirk.

"Not taking that bet," I laugh. "He's been twitchy ever since he picked them up."

I glance around the private jet's cabin and see Abra and Chaos in a deep discussion. I imagine they're talking about various means of torture. It makes me glad to be sitting back here with Pirate. Even if he is pissing me off. I'd rather be asleep like Zip, sitting behind us.

"Have you heard anything from your friend about the DNA results for the babies at the clubhouse?" Pirate asks.

"No. He said it would take him at least two weeks to get through all the samples. I'll only hear something if he finds a match early on. However, we don't know if the two babies came from any of the dead women. We don't know how long the women were in that building. The cops have only identified a few of them."

"Thirteen," Pirate corrects me. "They've identified thirteen of them. Just because they found empty cribs in the basement doesn't mean that's where Mikel acquired the babies."

I shrug. "Doesn't mean it isn't. The cops found two dirty diapers that weren't more than a few days old. I think Mikel took advantage of the ship sailing with all those kids to dispose of the babies and earn some money."

"Yeah, probably," Pirate mutters. "We need to find those assholes, because we know Mikel wasn't running that whorehouse alone. I want to tie them to a bed and ram a hot poker up their asses until they die."

"Shit, if I wanted an image like that, I'd go sit with Chaos and Abra," I complain.

Before Pirate can respond, our pilot, Maia, comes over the speaker to let us know that we'll be landing soon. Thank the Great Spirit.

An advantage to taking Angela Westbrook's private jet is that we could take our bikes. Jake arrived with the SUV and loads our suitcases. Dixie introduces his guests and our new prospects to Jake. With help from Pirate, Dixie smuggled two men from Ireland into the US, Conor Byrne and Danny Flynn. The two men are brothers, but Dixie's grandfather adopted Danny soon after Conor's arrest for participating in the theft that led to the death of Dixie's parents. Conor served his sentence but ran afoul of a gang leader in prison. Dixie brought them to the US to protect both men. Their arrival also helps us out. We need more prospects, especially after our previous prospect, Irish, betrayed us.

We say goodbye to Dante, Chaos, and Maia, who continue to San Diego.

As I mount my bike, my phone rings. The display shows it's my younger brother calling. Ignoring the call, I slide my phone back into my kutte. I can call him back once we're at the clubhouse. After Olivia has welcomed me home. Preferably naked.

Cleo and Delphine rush outside the clubhouse before we can park our bikes. Cleo flies into Hex's arms while Delphine walks calmly toward Dixie. I glance around, disappointed not to see Olivia. But then, I remember she's working a shift and sometimes can't leave on time. Dixie wraps Delphine in a hug and swings her around before kissing her. Then, without warning, he drops to his knee and proposes.

Pirate and I smirk at each other as my phone rings again. My brother. Again.

"What?" I answer.

"Is that any way to answer a phone?" he gripes.

"If you just called to check my phone etiquette, I'll save you the time. It sucks." I move my thumb to end the call, but he calls for me to wait.

"Lake, stop. I need your help. We need your help," he says.

"Did he tell you to call me?"

My brother's pause tells me what I already know.

"Look, you know how he is…"

"Yeah, an arrogant bastard who thinks he never needs help, least of all from his wastrel of a son."

Two-Feathers sighs, which sets off a twinge of guilt. My father's stubbornness isn't my brother's fault. He's been the unlucky buffer between my father and me for his entire life.

"What do you need?" I relent.

"Could you come for a visit? Some of our people need medical help, and you know how they are. They won't go to the hospital if they have a choice. We have two pregnant women who need ultrasounds. Some of the kids need their vaccinations. That sort of thing."

"What about the clinic?"

"That's something I need to talk to you about. Someone broke into the clinic and ransacked it. They sent the doctor to the hospital."

"Do you know who did it?"

"No one saw anything. The doctor was unconscious and can't tell us anything. Can you come?"

"Yeah, I can do that." I'm the unofficial Medicine Man for our tribe. Unofficial because our father, the Chief, won't acknowledge me.

"We also need to pick your brain," my brother continues. "I can't discuss it over the phone, but we need your help. I need your help."

"I don't know…" I start.

"Please. I wouldn't ask if it wasn't important or if I could handle it myself."

Knowing this is true, I consider relenting. "Has Dad acknowledged you as his successor yet, Toff?"

The pause is longer, and I can feel Toff's pain. "You know he hasn't. He still thinks you're going to come to your senses and take back your birthright."

"I'm not. You know that. Coyote knows it. He's just being an asshole. Look, I just got back and need to get some sleep. I'll come by tomorrow, and we'll talk. Let those who need medical help know to go to the clinic. For those who can't travel, I'll see them before I return home."

"Thanks," Toff says.

I end the call before he can say anything more.

Dreading the following day, I go inside and unpack before heading to the infirmary to prepare my medical bag. This doesn't take me long since I've made this trip too many times to count, although it has been a while. After they built the clinic, they didn't need me.

Glancing at my watch, I'm surprised Olivia hasn't sought me out. She must be home from her shift by now. I scan the common room but don't see her. A feeling of dread fills me as I seek out Levi.

"Have you spoken to Olivia?" I ask him.

"Yeah, earlier. I told her when you guys were due back. She was planning on being here when you arrived. Is she not here?"

"I can't reach her, and she's late. Was she going somewhere after work instead of back here?"

Levi glances around the room as he pulls out his phone. He calls her mobile but gets her voicemail. He dials again, and I hear him ask for Olivia. However, before they reply, I hear a noise behind me. Turning, I see a pale Delphine.

"Olivia," she whispers, leaning into Dixie. "She's in danger."

Chapter Two: Olivia

"Here you go, mama," I coo before placing the tiny, wriggling bundle in his mother's hands. The new mama shows all the signs of exhaustion one would expect after twelve hours of labor, but she smiles wide as she cuddles her newborn son.

"He's perfect, isn't he?" Abigail asks as she strokes her son's cheek. "Hello, Max."

"He is perfect. You do good work," I say with a grin. "You both do," I add when the muscular man beside her leans over and covers the baby's tiny head with his large hand.

"He's not the biological father. That asshole left me when I told him I was pregnant," Abigail says, her eyes on the man bent over her. "Steve is my hero. Our hero."

The man grins at her and softly kisses her temple. He shakes his head as he strokes Max's head.

"You both saved me," he says. His voice is rough with emotion and gravelly as if he doesn't use it often. "I'm just glad I was there when you needed me."

"What happened?" I ask, unable to stop myself.

"About two months ago, my car broke down on the way home from work. I was searching for my phone to call a tow truck when a white van pulled behind me. Two guys got out. They opened my door before I knew what was happening and pulled me out of the car. Steve came out of nowhere and took them both on. The men jumped back into their van and took off. I don't know what would have happened to us if he hadn't been there." She cups his cheek and stares into his eyes. He wraps his fingers around her wrist and lays his forehead against hers. Taking out my phone, I snap a picture.

"It's a good thing you were there," I say before showing them the picture I took. "You three make a good-looking family."

"Oh, I love it," Abigail says. "Can you send that to me?" She rattles off her phone number.

I send them the picture before helping the new mama breastfeed. Once Max has had his fill, I put him in the bassinet so Mama can rest.

"So, how has your first week been?" Sylvia asks me when I step up to the nurse's station. She's a few years older than me, with light brown hair and eyes that are the color of dark chocolate. Sylvia is a little on the pudgy side, but she's incredibly sweet.

I moved from Omega Hospital to Tulane five days ago. At Omega, I mainly worked with older patients who too often left our care to go into hospice. Dealing with those at the end of their lives had taken a toll on me, and I wanted something different. Besides, I needed to add to my experience as I worked toward my nurse practitioner certification. So, when the obstetrics position at Tulane came up, I applied for it and got it.

"I love it. Watching new life coming into the world has been uplifting, especially after my last position."

"That's what Talia said when she transferred over," Sylvia says. "She loved it here, which is why I don't get why she would just leave."

"You think she left?" I ask her. "I thought the police were investigating her disappearance as a kidnapping."

"Are they?" Joyce, who sits next to Sylvia, asks. Where Sylvia is sweet and approachable, Joyce is prickly. "A detective questioned us but said nothing about her being a kidnap victim. How do you know?"

"They questioned me, too, since we worked together for over a year." I lie. The cops did question me, but they never mentioned kidnapping. No, I'm the one who thinks Talia's disappearance was not her doing. I'm the one who suggested it to them.

"You guys worked together at Omega Hospital, right?" Sylvia asks.

I nod. "We did. I didn't know Talia was missing until I tried calling her to tell her about a patient we shared passing away."

"I thought you said you talked to the cops about her disappearance," Joyce says, narrowing her eyes.

"I did. I'm the one who suggested Talia's disappearance might be connected to Dr. Carver's," I explain.

"You think their disappearances are connected? Why?" Sylvia asks.

"Do you think it has something to do with them both transferring from Omega? Maybe someone doesn't like it when nurses and doctors leave Omega," Joyce offers. "You need to be careful."

She's likely joking, but I can't say I hadn't considered the connection. They both dated Dr. Calder, who works at Omega in pediatrics. He's dated almost every female nurse and doctor at the hospital. His dalliances last between one and two weeks. He tried it on with me before I left, but he backed off when I told him I was dating a motorcycle club member. I don't see him caring about either Marcia or Talia leaving Omega. He seemed pretty happy when they both left.

"I doubt their disappearances have anything to do with Omega. They didn't work in the same department until they transferred here," I say.

"But they both got dumped by the same doctor," Joyce smirks.

"That's right. Dr. Calder," Sylvia says. "Talia mentioned him. She said she wasn't surprised when he ghosted her. She knew their relationship had an expiration date. However, I remember Marcia was more upset. He pursued her after she told him she wasn't interested. He claimed that she was different, but of course, that was just a line. She was angry for falling for it, especially after she found out…" Sylvia's voice trails off.

"Found out what?" I ask.

"She wanted to keep it a secret, but it no longer matters. She's probably had it by now. Marcia was pregnant. She was four months along when she disappeared. The baby would be two months old by now."

Marcia was pregnant? "Was Dr. Calder the father?"

Sylvia shrugs. "I think so, but she didn't say only that the father was the world's biggest asshole. Which is the same thing she said about Dr. Calder."

I frown as I consider the ramifications. Would Dr. Calder be so despicable as to attack the mother of his child? He's a narcissist, but is he also a psychopath? My gut screams yes.

"She might have just left town to have the baby somewhere else," Joyce supplies.

"Wouldn't she have given notice first?" I ask. "She wouldn't just disappear. Neither of them would."

"I don't see Talia burning bridges. Although she's a good nurse and probably wouldn't have trouble finding another job. Marcia is a doctor. She wouldn't have to give notice. It isn't like they'd take her license. Maybe she wanted to set up a private practice somewhere else."

"I'm hoping they both found hot guys with lots of money who swept them off their feet," Sylvia says.

Joyce snorts. "You read too many romance novels. That would never happen in real life."

"Don't any of you have work to do?" Dr. Merkel asks.

"Sorry, doctor," Joyce simpers. I may have only been in the department for five days, but I know Joyce has a massive crush on the attractive doctor. His golden blonde hair is thick with a touch of a wave at the top. His sculpted cheekbones and straight nose create a handsome face, highlighted by his dark green eyes. I can understand her attraction, but he reminds me too much of Dr. Calder for him to do anything for me. However, Joyce pulls out all the stops when it comes to enticing Dr. Merkel. She's blonde, but I doubt it is her natural color. She also wears a tad too much makeup for her position. I don't wear much makeup as a rule, primarily because it is too much of a hassle. However, I've seen the reaction of new mothers around Joyce, especially when the eyes of the new fathers follow Joyce around the room, mainly because she wears her scrubs that are at least one size too small to enhance her ass and tits.

Checking my watch, I have another two hours before I can leave. The guys should be home by then. I can't wait to see Lake. He's only been gone two weeks, but I've missed him. Hell, I've missed all of them. The clubhouse has been eerily quiet with them gone. I know Cleo and Delphine have missed their men, too.

Those two hours fly by. I shower quickly, change into street clothes, and stuff my scrubs into a bag. My focus is only on seeing Lake again and welcoming him home. I'm thinking of the two of us naked in his bed, so I don't notice my car losing speed until I hear a horn blare behind me.

Jerking, I press the gas, but the car lurches before slowing down further. What the hell? Pulling to the side, the car behind me flies by. I see the one-finger gesture the driver gives me before he turns the corner and takes off. Jerk. Turning off the engine, I wait several seconds before trying the ignition. The clicking sound is not what I want to hear. What the hell? I just took the damn car in last month. What's going on?

I'm parked next to an empty park about three blocks from the hospital. The only lights come from the streetlamps. Apartment buildings surround me, but they look deserted. I don't spot a convenience store, gas station, or bar. Grabbing my purse, I dig around inside, looking for my phone. When I can't find it, I dump the contents on the seat, but still no phone. Where is my phone? I had it earlier when I photographed Abigail and her new family.

Abigail! Thinking about her reminds me of her story. How her car broke down, and two men tried to kidnap her. The cops found Talia's abandoned car, but not Talia. My gut screams to escape the vehicle and find a hiding place. Grabbing my keys and wallet, I yank open my door. When I slam it shut, I spot headlights passing by the entrance to the park. The van passes under a streetlamp—a white van heading directly toward me. I'm fucked!

Chapter Three: Lake

As Levi said, when I call Olivia's phone, it goes to voicemail. However, when I open the app that shows her location, I see that she's at Tulane Hospital.

"Her phone is at Tulane?" I ask Levi.

"She transferred over to Tulane a week ago. She got a position in obstetrics because she needs the experience for her nurse practitioner certification."

I'm disgruntled that she didn't mention changing jobs, but our phone calls while I was in Ireland with my brothers were more about checking in than long conversations. Since I couldn't share what we were doing, I didn't encourage her to fill me in on everything going on in her life. Now, I wish I had.

"Did you try calling the hospital to have them page her? Maybe her phone died," I suggest.

Levi just manages to keep from rolling his eyes. "I just called. They said she left about thirty minutes ago."

I move toward the door, intent on searching for her.

"Hold up, we'll go with you."

I see Dixie glance longingly at Delphine. He doesn't want to leave her.

"No, you should all go," Delphine says as Cleo nods. "She needs your help. We can celebrate when Olivia is home safe."

"You guys go. I'll crack into the hospital security feed. I'll also check the traffic cams if her car isn't there. Maybe she's driving home and accidentally left her phone at the hospital," Pirate offers, heading toward his office. "I'll call when I find her or if she arrives home."

The five of us hop on our bikes and ride through the gate. It feels fucking amazing to be back on my bike riding in the humidity after two weeks in a cold and wet country. I feel like I'm finally back home. The only thing that would make it perfect is if Olivia was my backpack. Usually, riding brings me peace, but I won't feel peace until we find her. My anxiety grows as we draw nearer to the hospital and haven't heard from Pirate. I thought we might pass her car on the way, but I know there are several routes she could have taken. I itch to shoot off by myself and search every possible route, but I fight my instincts. I settle in my spot next to Abra. Zip is in the lead as the Road Captain, with Hex and Dixie behind him and Abra and me taking up the rear. Zip will make sure we take the fastest route to the hospital.

Hex and the others search the hospital parking lot, leaving me to run inside to look for her. My first stop is obstetrics. Spotting a doctor, I approach him.

"Excuse me, I'm looking for Olivia Delacroix. Have you seen her?"

The doctor's eyes widened as he considered my size and kutte. He's tall, probably 6', but I'm several inches taller and broader. His doctor's coat, slacks, and button-down shirt fit his trim form, while my jeans and T-shirt don't hide my muscles.

"Who are you?" the doctor asks.

"I'm her man. Now tell me, have you seen her?"

"I saw her earlier, but her shift ended over an hour ago. Have you tried the staff locker room?"

"Where is it?"

He gave me directions to the second floor. I rushed down and found the room just as a nurse stepped out. "Excuse me, is there anyone else in there?"

"Someone is taking a shower."

"Can you check if it is Olivia Delacroix? I'm looking for her, but haven't found her. I'm her man. I just returned from Ireland and thought I'd surprise her at work."

"Oh, how sweet. Damn, Olivia is a lucky girl," the nurse says, eyeing me. "But she's not here. She left a while ago. I saw her going out to her car."

"Damn. Okay, thanks." I spin on my heel and run down the stairs to the lobby and back out the door. Hopping on my bike, I go in search of my brothers. When I find them, they're near the exit. Hex ends a call and glances at me.

"Pirate found Olivia on the traffic cams. He said she left the parking lot forty-five minutes ago."

I nod. This information matches what the nurse gave me. "Did he say which way she went?"

"Yeah, she was heading toward the clubhouse."

"Back the way we came? But we didn't see her." I feel panic rising, which is rare for me. I'm usually the calm one. Not knowing where Olivia is has me ready to tear out of my skin.

"Pirate is tracking her through the cams. Let's ride. He'll update us as he learns more. Calm down. We're going to find her," Hex assures me.

I nod, even though I want to rage at Hex. How can he suggest I calm down? If this were Cleo, he'd be riding through the streets screaming her name, which is what I want to do. But I don't. I have to trust Pirate. I have to trust my brothers. I joined the Demon Dawgs for a reason. We're a family, and we're stronger together. I can't cover all of New Orleans by myself. Pirate has the means to locate her, so I have to trust him to find her. Olivia needs me to stay calm and locate her, not go off the rails.

We're three blocks from the hospital before Zip pulls into an empty parking lot outside a public park. We follow him in before disembarking to join him. He's on the phone with Pirate. I can tell by Zip's question that Pirate lost Olivia.

Fuck!

I glance around the neighborhood. It's quiet, with no open businesses. Across the street is a row of apartment buildings. I see a couple of cameras, which I'm certain Pirate has accessed. I open my mouth to ask but spot a white van driving by. It's going slow. Too slow.

Abra tenses next to me. We both draw our guns as the van continues past us and turns at the nearby corner. I watch it as it continues its slow progress. It stops in the middle of the street for several seconds. I glance at Abra, who continues to watch the van. Opening my mouth to get Hex's attention, I spot a car in the van's headlights. A burgundy Honda Civic. Just like the one Olivia drives.

"That might be her car," I call out, returning to my bike.

The guys hop on theirs, and we rev our engines before easing back onto the road. When I pull in front of the parked car, the white van is gone. No one is in the front seat, but I see the silly cat ornament hanging from her rearview mirror. Its paws are up as if trying to get my attention. Well, it has it.

Swinging off my bike, I step to the driver's side door. My heart sinks when I yank on the handle and find it unlocked. Olivia wouldn't have willingly left her car door unlocked. Pushing the seat back, I slide in and check the ignition. No keys. Her purse sits on the passenger seat, surrounded by its contents. I see everything but her wallet and phone.

"Open the hood," Abra calls out. I do as he asks before restoring the items to her purse.

Where the fuck is she?

"Pirate, we found her car," Hex says, giving him the location before putting the phone on speaker.

"Okay, hold on, let me find the nearest traffic cam. Okay, I got it. It's on the corner. Let me see if it caught anything."

I glance down the street and spot the location. It's more than 200 feet away, so the chances of it catching anything we can use are minimal.

While waiting for Pirate to work his magic, Abra examines the engine.

"Someone fucked with her car," he says. "They knicked her radiator hose. Probably at the hospital. She'd get this far before the car died on her."

"Okay, got you. I can spot you on the camera, but barely. I'm rolling back the feed. Okay, here, I see where Olivia pulled over. Asshole." Pirate mutters.

"What? What happened?"

"Nothing. It looked like the car had lost power, so she pulled over to the side of the road. Some jerk had been riding her tail and flipped her off when he went past. Okay. I can see her moving in the car. She opened the door and got out. I think something spooked her. She took off running across the street. Damn, she's out of sight. I'll have to see if I can find her. Wait."

I growl. I don't want to fucking wait. I'm fucking tired of waiting. All I want to do is find Olivia and ensure she's okay.

"A van pulled behind her car, and two guys exited. At least, I think they're guys. I can't get a good look at them. Fuck, they took off after her."

Chapter Four: Olivia

"Oh shit, oh no," I mutter as I dart off the sidewalk and plaster my back to the side of the nearest building. Abigail's story and recalling how they found Talia's car broken down on the roadside sends me a chill. Are there men out there driving around and stopping at broken-down vehicles on the off-chance they find a woman they can grab?

Unwilling to make it easy for them, I slide over to a nearby hedge and duck down behind it. I watch the men open my car door. One searches my car before slamming the door shut. He pounds his fist into his hand in frustration. Both men look up and down the street before looking directly at me.

"Fuck. Just go away. Get into your van and drive off," I pray. But they don't listen. They continue to stare in my direction. Can they see me?

I glance down to see I'm in black slacks and a dark grey sweater. They shouldn't be able to see me in the shadows, but my heart speeds up when they walk towards me. I get a good look at them when they pass under a streetlamp. They're both wearing scrubs. Maybe they're from the hospital and stopped when they spotted the car? They could just be Good Samaritans, or perhaps they recognized my car. But then I realize they aren't just wearing scrubs but also surgical caps and masks as if going into surgery. Surgeons don't normally wear these outside the theater. They've covered their faces and hair. They're wearing these things to hide their identities. And they're headed straight for me.

I'm shaking. My reflexes scream to run, but I know I can't outrun them. Besides, I don't know where to run to. I see no hiding place or anyone who can help me. I consider running for the next street, but I'd be easy prey if it is as deserted as this one. I think of screaming, but will anyone care enough to come to my aid?

The two men stop several yards from where I'm hiding. They glance up and down the street.

"Where the fuck did she go? You think someone picked her up?"

"Who?"

"How the fuck would I know. They said she had a brother. Maybe she called him, and he picked her up."

"How the fuck could she have called him? We made sure she didn't have her phone."

I don't recognize their voices. They have southern accents, but not from Louisiana. Maybe Mississippi or Georgia? They seem to know about me, but I haven't met them. Maybe they work at the hospital? It would explain how they got ahold of the scrubs. They took my phone and know about my brother, so odds are they work at the hospital.

"Let's get back in the van and drive around. Maybe she walked back to the hospital, but we missed her."

I stay hidden behind the shrub, even as they drive off. I'm reluctant to give up my hiding place. What if they come back? There is no guarantee that I can find another place to hide. However, do I want to stay here all night? Levi must be worried. He'd know I was overdue. He'll probably come looking for me, especially after Lake and the others return. So, I know they'll be searching for me, but how long do I have to wait? Will they be able to find me?

I hear only silence, although I'm hoping for the roar of motorcycles. I leave my hiding place reluctantly. Staying in the shadows of the buildings and away from the streetlamps, I move away from my car. I'm only a few yards from the next street when I hear a sound that fills me with hope—the roar of a motorcycle, but not just one, several. The sound echoes off the buildings, making it hard for me to pinpoint their location.

If the riders are the Demon Dawgs, they'll look for my car. As I turn to go back, the engines cut off. I can see my car, but I don't see them. Where are they? Maybe it wasn't them. Another club?

I'm standing on the sidewalk when the sound of a motor cuts through the silence. I see the white van pull behind my car. Shit! Shit! Shit! Do I move or stay still? I hope they don't look this way. If I move, they may see the movement and come to investigate. Holding my breath, I watch in relief as the van pulls out and continues down the street. Knowing I must stay out of sight, I return to the shadows. That's when I hear several engines rev. Motorcycles. Could it be?

Staying next to the building, I wait and pray. Relief floods through me when five motorcycles circle my car. I recognize the one who jumps off his bike first and opens my door. Lake. I'd recognize that man anywhere. How could I not? Whenever he enters a room, my eyes go to him. The Demon Dawg members are all exceptionally hot, but Lake is not only hot; he's exotic with his Native American heritage. He wears his long black hair loose. His skin is a rare reddish-copper color that glows like polished wood. His dark brown eyes carry the wildness of his ancestry. It's easy to picture him shirtless, wearing deerskin leggings, and riding a horse. He's a fantasy come to life.

I shake myself from my lustful thoughts. They are not helping me escape danger. Standing, I dash into the street, waving my arms while yelling for Lake. My focus is on him. I don't want them to hop on their bikes and leave me behind. However, I don't consider that I might attract the attention of the two men chasing me. I hear a motor approaching from behind. Spinning, I see the white van barrelling toward me. Screaming louder, I run faster toward the men I know will protect me.

However, the van catches up to me. Swerving to block my path, I try to dodge around, but the door opens, and a man steps out and lunges at me.

"Olivia, drop!" Lake bellows.

I react without thinking and drop to the ground. Bullets fly over my head. I don't look up until I hear a car door slam. The van pulls away while Hex and his men keep shooting. Lake drops next to me and pulls me into his arms.

"I've got you, baby. You're safe. Did they hurt you?" he asks as he searches my body for damage.

"I banged my right knee on the tarmac and have gravel on my hands and knees. Otherwise, I'm fine." I wrap my arms around my hero and let my body melt into his. Unable to keep them from falling, tears trail down my cheeks and onto his kutte. I've never been so scared, not even when the men seeking revenge against Levi ambushed me.

"Let's get you back to the clubhouse," Lake says, standing with me in his arms. I should protest about him carrying me, but I can't do it. I need to feel safe, and that's how he makes me feel. Safe.

He places me on his bike before cleaning off my hands and pants. "I'll look at your knee when we're back at the clubhouse."

I nod. My knee is throbbing. It needs cleaning and some ice.

"Do you have your keys?" Abra asks. I take them out of my pocket and hand them over. "The fuckers messed with your car. I've called for a tow truck."

"I'll grab your purse," Lake offers.

"Thank you."

"Did you recognize those men?" Hex asks me.

I shake my head. "They were dressed like doctors going into surgery. They had the scrubs, masks, and caps. I heard them speaking, but I didn't recognize their voices. Although, I think I'd recognize them."

"You think they work at the hospital?"

"Maybe. One of them mentioned taking my phone. I had my phone while I was working. I only didn't have it on me when showering in the nurse's lounge. Since they were in scrubs, they could walk around the hospital without anyone noticing. Come to think of it, their disguise was a good one. The masks and the caps hide their faces and cover their hair. Anyone who saw them outside the hospital would assume they were doctors on their way home."

"Do you think they targeted you?" Hex asks. Lake hisses at him when he hands me my purse.

I place a hand on Lake's arm to keep him from snapping at his President. "I know they targeted me. They mentioned Levi. Not by name, but mentioned I had a brother. One said he took care of my phone. I couldn't find my phone when my car stalled. It's why all my crap was all over the passenger seat. I was looking for it. I knew I had it earlier."

"The phone is showing up at the hospital," Lake tells me.

"All roads lead back to the hospital," Hex says.

Chapter Five: Lake

"Shit!" I explode as I glance at my brothers. Each stared at me in horror after Pirate's update. "What happened next? Did they catch up to her?"

"Hold on, no. The two men came back to the van alone and took off. I'm fast-forwarding until you get there. Wait, the van came back and stopped next to her car. Then it took off again. Okay, now I see you guys arrive. Maybe she's hiding?"

"Or maybe they caught up to her. Keep looking. Check other cameras."

"On it," Pirate says before ending the call.

Where would she go? I see movement down the side street perpendicular to us. Someone is running toward us, their arms waving.

"Olivia!" I shout as I run toward her. I hear the engine first, then see the white van round the corner. It's behind Olivia and coming up fast. I scream at her to get out of the way, but she freezes when the van pulls up alongside her.

The five of us palm our guns as we run toward the van. When the doors open and two men step out, I shoot high to avoid hitting Olivia, who stands frozen even as the man grabs her arm.

I yell for her to drop. Which, gratefully, she does. With her safely out of range, we unload on the van. The echoes of gunfire and the pings of bullets hitting metal fill the air. The windshield cracks, and we blow out both headlights, eliminating the light. The men dive back into the van. We continue shooting as they back up into the cross street before taking off.

The others continue to rush forward while I drop next to Olivia. Gathering her in my arms, I hold her quaking body. "I've got you, baby. You're safe. Did they hurt you?"

Luckily, her injuries are slight. They mainly occurred when she fell to the ground. I'll give her an exam once we're back at the clubhouse. But first, we need to deal with her car. Abra and Zip offer to stay behind and get Olivia's car towed. Abra's quick exam of the engine confirmed our fear. Someone tampered with her car. The assholes knew she wouldn't get far before the car broke down. This means they could have only tampered with it when she was at work. As Hex aptly stated, all roads lead to the hospital.

Back at the clubhouse, Levi is the first outside to meet us. Delphine and Cleo are a few steps behind him. Levi hugs his sister and refuses to relinquish her to the women. So, they wrap themselves around the siblings.

"We were so worried about you," Delphine says, stroking Olivia's hair.

"You saw I was in danger?" Olivia asks. Delphine nods. Delphine has a gift. She can sense when someone she cares about needs help. She's never been wrong, so we never dismiss her premonitions. Even before Olivia entered our lives, Delphine sensed Olivia was in danger, sending us off to rescue her. I'll forever be grateful for Delphine's visions. They brought Olivia into my life and helped us rescue her tonight.

"I need to take care of our girl," I tell them, breaking through the huddle and drawing out my woman.

Levi reluctantly releases her. I can see he wants to argue with me. He likely thinks I want to play doctor with my beautiful nurse. I do, but that's not what is happening right now. "She hurt her knee when she dodged the men who tried to kidnap her," I tell him. "We won't be long. I'm sure Olivia is hungry."

"Starved," Olivia agrees, squeezing her brother's arm. "I'm okay. We'll only be a few minutes."

When Hex took possession of the neglected plantation, I suggested we turn one room into an infirmary. I'd seen the decked-out space Scar created in the San Diego clubhouse and wanted something similar. Gratefully, Hex agreed. Now, I have an exam room with two tables instead of just one. I knew the likelihood of an incident putting one brother on his back would involve another brother. We always had each other's backs and wouldn't hesitate to jump in when another was under attack.

Hex gave me three rooms for my plan. One contained the exam tables, another the supplies, and the third had two beds for anyone needing recovery. I lifted Olivia onto the table. Under the bright lights, I can see the damage.

"I'm cutting off the pants," I tell her. "They're ruined."

She nods as she glances at the dress pants with a sizeable hole in the knee. Grabbing a pair of scissors, I cut them off just above the knee. There isn't much blood but plenty of gravel. Picking up a pair of tweezers, I carefully remove the pieces from her knee and palms before cleaning them.

I kiss her knee before wrapping it with gauze and then kiss her palms. She places her palms on my face before pulling me forward for a kiss.

"I'm okay," she whispers against my lips.

Remembering the fear I felt when I saw the van barrel down on her has me crushing my lips against hers. Wrapping my arms around her, I plaster my body against hers. Knowing she's safe is the only thing keeping me from rushing out of the clubhouse and hunting down those assholes. I know we need to find and stop them, but taking care of Olivia is all that matters now.

"We're going to figure out who they are," I tell her.

She nods. "I know. But for right now, I need you to hold me. And feed me."

I chuckle when her stomach growls in agreement. Care first, violence later.

"After I change," she says, sliding off the exam table and glancing at herself.

She jogs upstairs while I find Hex. He and the rest of my brothers are sitting at the table. I can smell something amazing coming out of the kitchen. I pull out the chair next to Abra's.

"We were just talking about what Abra saw under Olivia's hood. They messed with her radiator line, the same tactic they used on Talia's car."

I nod, unsurprised at the news. "They must have tampered with both cars while the women were on shift."

"I've tried accessing the security feed, but Tulane has a better than decent firewall. I need to get closer and work some magic," Pirate adds.

"What about her phone? Is it still pinging at the hospital?"

Pirate nods.

"I overheard them say they took care of my phone," Olivia says as she slides into the seat beside mine. "I know I had the phone while I was working. They must have stolen it from my locker when I was in the shower. It's the only time I didn't have it on me."

"That gives us a good window," Pirate says. "If I can access the security feed, I can see who went in and out of the locker room. That might give us our targets."

"I could go to security and ask them to check the feed," Oivia offers. "I can tell them someone stole my phone. Which is true."

"I don't like the idea of you going back there," I say, sliding my arm over her shoulders and drawing her closer.

"I can't avoid going back. I work there now. At least I know I'm in danger. I'll be alert."

"Since I'll be driving you to work, following you around, and then driving you home again, you're right. You won't be in danger again."

Olivia snorts as if I was joking. I'm not. No way am I letting her out of my sight again. Not until we figure out the identity of these assholes and put them six feet under.

"Okay, caveman," Olivia says, patting my chest. "We can discuss my safety later. I'm off for the next four days."

Hearing that calms me down. I don't want to fight with Olivia, but if she thinks I won't follow through with my plan to keep her safe, she'll soon figure out I mean what I say. "Does that mean you agree not to go in tomorrow to get your phone? Pirate and I can go. We'll search the locker room for it."

Olivia frowns. "I don't think they'll let you in. It's a woman's locker room."

"How about the three of us go?" Cleo offers. "Safety in numbers. If anyone asks, we are simply three friends going out shopping. Olivia wanted to stop at the hospital because she left her phone. Delphine and I can watch for anyone paying her too much attention."

Olivia nods at the suggestion, and I find I'm not against it, especially if they have us as backup. "I'll agree if we all go. We can wait for you in the lobby. Might be good for whoever tried to kidnap you to know you have our club behind you."

"Don't you think they got that message when you shot at them?" Olivia asks with a smirk.

"Which reminds me. I called several body shops and told them to contact me if someone brought the van in for work. Although, I imagine they'll ditch the van. It's what I would do," Abra says.

Chapter Six: Olivia

I find that fleeing for my life gives me an appetite. Who knew hiding from kidnappers could do that? It didn't hurt that Nora made one of my favorite comfort foods, baked mac and cheese. It's almost like she knew I'd need the scrumptious, cheesy goodness to wipe out the fear.

As we eat, I glance around the table. Having the men back makes the meal noisier than when only Cleo, Delphine, and I sat down together. The noisiness calms me. I'm safe here. Lake and his brothers are better than any locked door, security system, or guard dog. No one could get me here. If I had gone through today and spent the night in my apartment, I know I'd never have gotten any sleep. As I finish my food, I know I'll crash soon. I hope I can stay asleep.

"Tired?" Lake asks, jolting me. I hadn't realized I'd been dozing.

"I am."

"Let's go to bed."

"Remember Church in the morning, and then we'll go to the hospital," Hex reminds Lake.

"I'll be there," Lake assures him as he pulls me out of my chair and wraps his arm around my waist. I lean on him as we take the stairs to the second floor. Lake's room is nearest the stairs. Something I'm most grateful for tonight.

Once in his room, he locks the door before helping me undress. When I'm naked, he lifts the covers so I can slide in. A few seconds later, I feel Lake slide in behind me. He pulls me toward him so my leg is over his, and my head rests on his chest. One hand rests on my ass while he clasps my hand with the other. Feeling safe and cared for, I drift off.

Hands grab me, yanking me out of my car. I see a surgeon standing nearby, a scalpel in his hand, as his accomplice drags me into the back of a van. Inside, I see blood everywhere. Pools of blood on the floor, splattered on the walls, but the ceiling, fuck, the ceiling. Blood drips onto the floor. I struggle to get away, but the man pushes me into the van and onto the floor. I'm rolling around in blood, feeling it drip on my body, my arms, and my face. I want to scream, but I'm scared of the blood going into my mouth. Then, the level of blood rises.

"Olivia, wake up! Baby, wake up! You're having a nightmare. Come back to me."

Lake's frantic words bring me back to consciousness. I reach out to him, trying to comfort him, only to find him holding me so tightly I can't move. "Lake," I mumble.

"I'm here, baby. You're here. We're in my room. You're safe."

I focus on Lake's voice and pry my eyes open. I'm staring into his dark orbs. We're so close I can see myself reflected there.

"I'm okay. I'm awake. It was just a bad dream. Blood. So much blood. A surgeon with a scalpel." I shake the image away. "Just a dream."

"I couldn't reach you," Lake says, his voice still holding a hint of panic. "You went rigid, and then you started fighting me. I couldn't get you to calm down."

"I'm sorry," I say, which makes him chuckle.

"You have nothing to be sorry for, silly girl. You can't control your nightmares. Do you want to go back to sleep? It's only two in the morning."

I did want to go back to sleep, but there was something I wanted more. Sliding out of Lake's hold, I slide until I'm at eye-level with his glorious cock. After licking off the pre-cum, I lick along the vein, which pulses under my administration. Lake groans as I massage his balls with my left hand while stroking his cock with my right. He goes from hard to steel rod when I slide the tip inside my mouth. I feel powerful and in control, which clears away the remnants of the nightmare.

"Fuck, baby, you're so good at that," Lake mutters as he slides his fingers through my hair.

I lower my mouth until his dick pokes the back of my throat. Using my hand to pump and my mouth to slide over his generous length, I feel my core weep at the grunts and moans he makes. There is something about giving pleasure to your man that gets the juices flowing.

Taking a deep breath, I suck him hard and deep. His grip tightens painfully in my hair as he holds me in place. His dick slides down my throat as his hips surge forward. The lack of oxygen makes me lightheaded, but I swallow around him, which makes him groan loudly. He pulls me away so his cock slides out with a pop. I'm ready to retake him, but he shifts me until I'm hovering over his waiting cock.

"I need to come inside you. I need to feel you," Lake says as he lowers me until he pierces my core.

Fuck, yeah! This is what I need, too. "Oh, baby, fuck me. Fuck me hard. Make me forget," I moan as he jerks his hips and slams me down, impaling me on his cock. My core wraps tightly around him, drawing him in.

The ride is rough but with enough tenderness to touch my soul. He slides in and out of me, building my orgasm until it washes over me in waves of pleasure. Collapsing on his chest, I kiss his sternum as he strokes my back.

"Can we stay here, just like this?" I ask him.

He palms my ass with one hand while still stroking my back with the other. "I think that's one of your best ideas."

We can't stay joined forever, but that doesn't stop us from drifting back to sleep with our bodies intimately connected.

I wake to an empty bed, but he's left a note.

'Gone to Church. I'll meet you for breakfast.'

Smiling, I climb out of bed and into the shower. There is nothing hotter than a man who communicates. After getting dressed, I head downstairs to find Cleo and Delphine drinking coffee while waiting for their men. I duck into the kitchen to grab a mug and breathe in the glorious scent of French Toast and bacon.

"That smells amazing," I tell Nora, who places her spatula down before hugging me.

"I heard about yesterday. I'm so glad they found you."

Even though Nora is one of the Kutte Bunnies, she feels more like part of the family. All the Kutte Bunnies do. Abra, Pirate, and Zip sometimes hook up with the girls, but I've never felt like they're competition. Lake may have hooked up with one or two of them before me, but neither the women nor Lake allude to it. Like Nora, the other Kutte Bunnies stay here for free with the understanding they help out around the clubhouse. I never get the feeling that sex is a condition for their staying.

Wrapping my hands around the mug of coffee, I sit next to Cleo and across from Delphine. The sparkling green emerald on Delphine's finger catches my eye when she picks up her coffee. Almost dropping my mug, I grab her hand.

"What's this?"

Delphine chuckles. "Dixie proposed to me the minute they arrived home. The ring belonged to his mother. He had it in a safe deposit box in Ireland and brought it home for me."

"You're engaged? Congratulations. God, I'm so sorry he had to leave you and come help me."

"Nonsense," Delphine chides me. "Of course, he had to go rescue you. You're family. I'm just glad they got to you in time. Besides, we celebrated most of the night." Her self-satisfied smirk is enough to reassure me that I didn't stop them from consummating their engagement.

"When is the wedding?"

"We haven't set a date yet. I'm hoping soon. I'm not getting any younger. Although I want both sons there, I'll have to wait for Vladimir to return from Russia."

"Have you heard from him?" Cleo asks.

Vladimir is Hex's twin brother. Their father stole Vladimir from the hospital while Hex and Delphine were recovering from a difficult birth. The bastard let her see Vladimir once a year until he turned eighteen, then stopped all visits. She thought she had lost him forever, but Vladimir is now back in her life. He, along with the Demon Dawgs, came to our rescue when Delphine's ex-husband kidnapped us along with Delphine's daughters. He intended to give Delphine and the girls as a gift to some Bratva big wig for his birthday. At the same time, Cleo and I would provide entertainment for his men on the voyage. I shudder at the memory.

"He called me when the ship landed. I haven't heard from him since. But he said he would contact me when he could. He's playing a dangerous game but seems confident he'll win."

Nora opens the kitchen door to bring out the food as the men come through from Church.

Chapter Seven: Lake

I untangle myself from Olivia without waking her. She burrows deeper under the covers, snagging my pillow and burying her face. Smiling, I duck into the bathroom for a quick shower before heading downstairs for Church.

I find Abra and Pirate filling their mugs with coffee in the kitchen. I take the pot once Pirate's done and pour myself some. I have a feeling I'm going to need it today. Olivia's nightmare kept me awake for hours after I fucked her into unconsciousness. I want to find those bastards who scared her and gave her that fucking nightmare.

"You look rough," Pirate says after I take a few chugs of coffee before topping off my mug again. "Bad night? Did Olivia have nightmares?"

I nod and tell him what I overheard her crying out in her sleep as she thrashed.

"Fuck. Poor thing. Hopefully, when we find and end these assholes, she'll sleep better."

"I found out some things that could help us. Although, they might freak Olivia out more," Abra adds.

"Ready?" Hex asks, poking his head into the kitchen.

The three of us follow him to the meeting room, where we hold our meetings. A table with our club logo etched in the center dominates the room. The six of us take up only half the space. Hex has plans to expand our ranks now that Dixie has struck a lucrative deal with Sigil.

Sigil is a private organization that offers assassinations for a hefty price. Dixie has worked for them his entire adult life. A fact he only shared with us recently. When Sigil contacted Dixie about a hit on Hex's brother, Vladimir, Dixie came clean with us. We helped him fake Vladimir's death. When Sigil learned of this, they called Dixie back to Ireland. We went with him as backup, but we were unnecessary.

It turned out Sigil didn't mind that Dixie faked Vladimir's death. Although, they didn't explain why. Groups like theirs don't have to explain. If I had to guess, they didn't want to lose Dixie as an operative. Especially since belonging to an MC, Dixie gains added protection and a layer of anonymity most assassins would, well, kill for. Sigil made us an offer we couldn't refuse. Assist Dixie in his tasks, and Sigil will keep our coffers full. Something that makes particularly happy since I'm the Treasurer.

Once we're all seated, Hex starts the meeting.

"We'll get to the heavy stuff in a minute, but let's go through the basics first. How are we looking?" He directs this question to me.

I haven't had much time to work the books since we landed back in the States, but luckily, I had caught up on the plane ride home.

"Sigil came through with their first payment. It's in the books as a deposit for a security consultant. The account they use to pay us is a personal security business. They're producing paperwork to prove they've hired us as temporary security guards, which they'll use as needed. It should be enough to fool the IRS. The bar, the tattoo parlor, and the auto shop are all in the black."

"We need another business or two," Hex says. "Know we don't have the manpower, but as we bring on more prospects, I want businesses for them to work in."

"We could start a security business," Pirate suggest. "Byte and Smoke make bank in San Diego with theirs. It would help if we found a prospect like Maestro."

Hex snorts. Maestro, a prospect with the main Chapter of the Demon Dawgs, is a computer savant. Finding him was a stroke of luck for their club.

"Reaper started a gun club. We could do that here. We could start small and build up as we take on more prospects," Abra adds.

We don't have to wait until we get more prospects," Zip chimes in. "Nora's close to graduating from culinary school. We could set her up with a restaurant that she could run. Maybe offer her a partnership?"

"A good idea. I'll talk to Nora. We could use the money from Sigil to get her established if she's interested. In the meantime, Jack has asked his brother to come out here to give us a bid on converting the old slave quarters into a guest clubhouse. Jack thinks some of his brother's guys would be interested in prospecting for us," Hex says.

As Secretary, Pirate documents the plan before we move on to the next topic—the attack on Olivia and the missing women.

"Pirate, did you see who messed with Olivia's car?" Hex asks.

"No, I can't get through the hospital firewall. If I can get inside the hospital, I can put in a backdoor. I tracked the van after you scared them off. They drove into a neighborhood, and I lost them. Figured I'd drive around the area and hack into doorbell cams to see if I can spot them."

"Did you find out anything?" Hex asks Abra.

Abra nods. "Yep, same MO that they used to sabotage Talia's car. This method is effective. They knick the radiator hose just enough for the liquid to drain out slowly. The car starts fine, and the driver gets about three blocks before the car conks out. I have some feelers to local chop shops to see if anyone snagged the doctor's sweet ride. I think that's why the cops couldn't find it. My guess is they follow this pattern. The question is how they gain access to the cars without anyone being the wiser."

"If they got into the locker room to grab her phone, maybe they grabbed her keys, too."

"Olivia had her keys," I remind them.

"Once I have access to the security feed, we can find out what happened," Pirate says.

"We're still no closer to understanding why they targeted these women. They all work in obstetrics. Could that be the link?" Dixie asks.

"Just because we know about the kidnapping of these three women doesn't mean they are the only three. Have you checked the police database to see if they've found a link to other victims," Hex suggests.

"I'll make it happen," Pirate says.

"How is Olivia? Did she remember anything else to help identify the men?" Hex asks me.

"She had a nightmare," I tell them about her seeing blood and surgeons. "She didn't recognize their voices, although she thought they weren't from here but the Deep South. She made a good point about how they dressed. As someone in the medical field, she knows surgeons don't typically wear their gear in public. But, even as a medical professional, she first thought they might have been from the hospital. She almost gave up her cover to wave them down. Imagine if these guys approached a layperson?"

"They'd assume the men were trustworthy. Shit," Abra says. "Clever. Beats the hell out of black clothes and a ski mask."

"Whoever they are, they have access to the gear. They also feel comfortable walking into the nurse's locker room to steal their victim's phones. This was a well-thought-out plan. They knew which car belonged to Olivia."

"They also knew she had a brother. So, they know their victims. I just don't know how she got on their radar," I say.

"She transferred over to Omega from Tulane, like the other victims. Maybe that's the connection?" Zip offers.

"I can access the staff records for Omega. I can check for anyone born or living in the south before moving to Louisiana," Pirate says. "I'll do the same when I get into Tulane's records. Maybe someone targets recent transfers because the staff may think they just took off?"

"We're looking at someone familiar with both hospitals and their staff," Hex confirms. "We'll start our search there. Anything else?"

"Yeah, I've got something. I know the timing is bad, but my brother called. He needs me to come home and provide medical assistance to the tribe. Someone destroyed their clinic and roughed up the doctor who operated it. They have two pregnant women who need ultrasounds and exams, along with kids who need vaccines. I can try to postpone for a few days if you need me to be around. However, Olivia is off for the next four days. I was thinking of taking her with me. Maybe a change of scenery will help."

"Plus, it will keep the assholes from finding her," Abra says.

"Good idea," Hex says. "You'll only be a few hours away if we need you back here. Who took out the clinic? Kids or someone causing trouble for the tribe?"

"I don't know. I plan on asking Toff about it when I see him. He didn't tell me much over the phone, but I know him. He sounded worried about something."

"Let us know if there is more going on than just an isolated case of vandalism," Hex says. "We may have our hands full with these assholes kidnapping women, but the tribe is your family, too. We'll be there if you need us."

Chapter Eight: Olivia

Before I met Lake, I never saw myself riding on the back of a motorcycle. They were death traps—donor cycles. So, I was unprepared for the first time I climbed behind Lake. Unprepared for the feeling of freedom. I was certainly unprepared to enjoy it as much as I did. There is something intimate about wrapping yourself around your man, feeling the throbbing machine between your legs, and the sexiness of watching him easily control the powerful machine. My analytical mind knows that we're one careless driver away from death, but I still feel safe riding behind Lake.

Much too soon, we pull up at Tulane Hospital. Cleo and Delphine climb off their men's bikes to join me as we enter the hospital lobby. The guys come in behind us but sit to wait for us while I take the girls up to the second floor.

I go straight to my locker and check inside. Since I've only worked there for a week, I haven't had much time to accumulate too many things. I have travel-size bottles of soap, shampoo, conditioner, and an extra pair of scrubs. As I expected, I didn't find my phone. The girls and I search the locker room. Lockers line the walls with benches in between. We searched under the benches and tried each locker with no luck.

"Try calling her phone," Cleo suggests to Delphine. "Maybe whoever took it didn't turn it off."

Delphine takes out her phone and makes the call. We hear a phone ring and follow the sound to the laundry cart outside the shower. The cart is half full of damp towels and dirty scrubs. Digging through them to the bottom of the cart, my hand brushes over something hard. Grabbing it, I pull out my phone.

The door to the nurse's lounge opens, and Joyce steps in. Her eyes go wide when she spots Cleo and Delphine. I'm guessing she's wondering why two biker chicks wearing property kuttes are in the lounge.

"Hi, Joyce."

Her eyes snap to me and widen further. "Olivia? What are you doing here? I thought you were off for a few days."

"I am, but I lost my phone. The last time I had it was at the hospital, so I returned to look for it." I show her my phone before stepping over to the hand sanitizer dispenser. I pump out a couple of dollops, which I use to sanitize my hands and my phone.

"You found it? That's good. I've lost my phone once or twice. What a pain. I once dropped it in the laundry cart with my scrubs and a towel. I didn't realize what I'd done until the next day. Luckily, I got back here just as they were wheeling out the cart," Joyce says before moving to her locker and pulling out her purse. "Is that what happened to you?"

"No. I didn't put anything in the cart, so I do not know how it happened. Look, Joyce, you and the other nurses need to be careful. Someone tampered with my car last night, so I broke down a few blocks from here. Two men wearing scrubs and masks arrived in a van. They were looking for me. I hid and managed to avoid them before my friends showed up."

Joyce's eyes grow wider as I tell her my story. Then she shakes her head. "Are you sure they weren't just doctors stopping to offer their help? Why would they try to kidnap you?"

"Someone tampered with her car," Cleo says. "The same way someone tampered with Talia's car. Possibly Marcia's as well."

Joyce narrows her eyes at Cleo. I can see the argument forming in her mind. "Joyce, they almost ran me down, and they tried to drag me into the van. They would have succeeded if it wasn't for the Demon Dawgs."

"The Demon Dawgs?" Joyce looks at me, her eyes going wide again. She's certainly giving them a workout.

Cleo turns so Joyce can see the club logo on the back of her property kutte. "Demon Dawgs. My man is Hex. He's the President and

Delphine's son. Delphine is with Hex's vice president, Dixie. Olivia is with Lake."

"You don't have on a vest," Joyce says.

"Lake and I have only been together for a few weeks. He hasn't claimed me."

"Yet," adds Delphine. "Soon, though."

While I want to believe she's right, I can't think about it now. I need to ensure Joyce understands the danger she and the rest of the nurses face. "Just be careful, okay? If you break down, get out of your car and hide. Maybe carpool with other staff members if you can. I don't know how they disabled my car, so I can't tell you what to look for under the hood."

Joyce shrugs. "I wouldn't know what I was looking for. Okay, I'll be careful. Did you tell the cops?"

"Not yet, but I will. I don't want what happened to Talia and Marcia to happen to you or others. So be vigilant."

Joyce nods as we leave her standing by the nurse's lounge.

"Maybe I should tell security what happened," I muse.

"Let's talk to the guys first," Delphine says. "You can always call security later and tell them what happened."

"Why not now?"

"Because they might be in on it," Cleo says. "If they know you suspect your attackers tampered with your car here or were responsible for hiding your phone, then they might erase the camera footage."

I nod at her reasoning. A few days won't matter, right?

I sure hope not.

"Did you find your phone?" Lake asks when we join the men.

I hold it up so he can see it. "Found it in the laundry cart. But I know I didn't drop it in there."

He nods. "Whoever took it didn't want anyone to find it on their person. They likely dropped it in there to hide it; if the cops found it, it would appear like you accidentally dropped it. Smart."

"I told a nurse I work with about the attack. I hope that's okay. I just wanted to warn her in case the assholes try again. I should tell security, but Cleo suggested they might be in on it. Looking the other way when they tamper with the car."

"She might be right. Whoever the fuck these guys are probably need someone in security to watch their backs. If Pirate gains access to their network, he can search the video, see who was on security then, and run him."

"Are we headed back to the clubhouse now?"

"We're stopping for lunch first. Pirate wants to double-check his access before we get back there."

The restaurant we stop at is only a few blocks from the hospital. It's charming and has a French Quarter feel. A wrought-iron fence surrounds a pretty outdoor seating area, and diners fill most tables even in cooler weather. We follow Cleo and Hex inside the restaurant. Cleo glances around as if looking for someone.

"Cleo, my beautiful angel, you've been away far too long!" The man who approaches us is tall and almost painfully thin. He wears his long dark hair pulled back into a sleek tail that falls down his back. His eyes are a clear blue. He's wearing a silk suit the color of smoke, a shirt that matches his eyes, and a maroon tie. He sweeps Cleo up into a hug and swings her around. He puts her on her feet seconds after Hex's loud growl. Hex pulls Cleo back into his arms and glowers at the man. Hex's reaction makes the man chuckle. "I see you've found yourself a caveman—good for you, Princess Cleo. You deserve someone who appreciates you. Do not worry, Mr. Caveman. Cleo is like the daughter I never had. My name is Francois, and I own this restaurant."

Hex shakes Francois' hand reluctantly. Francois beams at him before glancing at our group. "Nine for lunch? Outside, or would you like to stay in where it is warmer?"

"You know I always eat outside," Cleo says. "You wouldn't happen to have…"

"Your favorite spot? Of course. I save it only for the people I like. Therefore, it is almost always available."

Cleo laughs as Francois leads us outside the restaurant onto the patio. However, he doesn't stop until he reaches a section hidden from view behind a wrought-iron fence covered in magnolias and wisteria. We pass through an archway before he stops at the single table large enough to accommodate our group.

"Here is the menu, but I hope you will let me choose for you," Francois says once we're seated.

"You choose, Francois. You've never let me down."

Chapter Nine: Lake

I chuckle at Hex's expression when Cleo compliments Francois. We're all jealous fuckers when it comes to our women. We don't like them noticing other men exist, much less complimenting them.

"I'll place your order," Francois says, smirking at Hex's obvious irritation. "I hear little Nora is close to graduating. Michael will be sad to see her leave."

"How do you know Nora?" Abra asks, glaring at Francois.

"My husband Michael is her teacher at the culinary school. He feels like a father to that little girl. I've offered her a position here once she graduates."

I frown at his comment. Only this morning did we discuss setting up a restaurant for Nora as another source of income for the club. None of us considered she might have other options that she's pursuing. I glance at Dixie and nod. If we want to keep Nora, we should talk to her soon.

"We're very proud of her, too," Delphine tells Francois. "We're also very grateful to have been her taste testers."

When Francois leaves, Hex turns to Dixie. "We should talk to Nora when we return to the clubhouse." Dixie nods.

"Talk to her about what?" Delphine asks.

"We were discussing new business opportunities during Church. We thought we'd see if Nora wanted to partner with us in opening a new restaurant. The club needs more income, and I know a restaurant with her as head chef would do well."

"That's a great idea!" Cleo exclaims. "I think she'd jump at the opportunity. It's something she's always wanted. Let's hurry up and eat so we can return to the clubhouse. I can't wait to work with her! We can look for a good location and then get everything set up. Oh, this is going to be so much fun!"

Hex smirks at Cleo when she pulls out her phone and gets busy.

"What are you doing?" Hex asks her.

"I'm contacting my realtor. He needs to find us some properties to look at."

"Don't you think we should talk to Nora first?" Delphine asks with a chuckle.

Cleo's crestfallen expression has Hex sending a dirty look toward his mother.

"It won't hurt for you to have him get started," Hex tells Cleo.

"No, Delphine's right. We need to talk to Nora first. But I'm certain she'll say yes. I know how much she loves you guys. She'll be thrilled to know how much confidence you have in her. Besides, we should probably discuss the type of restaurant we want to open before we start looking at locations."

"You're opening a restaurant?" Francois asks, coming into the courtyard carrying two plates. Behind him are a series of waitstaff carrying food and drinks. Francois lays one plate in front of Cleo and the other in front of Hex. At the same time, his staff serves everyone else. Once the staff leaves, Cleo explains.

"We're talking about the Demon Dawgs investing in a restaurant," Cleo explains. "The club already owns a bar. They think a restaurant would be a good investment."

Francois nods. "It can be. I'd be interested in selling if you were looking for an established restaurant. Or, if you wanted to invest."

Cleo looks scandalized. "Why? You've owned this restaurant since I was a kid."

He waves his hands to stop Cleo from asking questions. "I shouldn't have mentioned it. Now is not the time to discuss business. Now is the time to eat and enjoy your food. We can talk later. Please, enjoy your meal."

Once Francois leaves, Cleo picks up her fork but only toys with her food.

"Eat," Hex orders her.

She eats a few bites while we dig into our meal. It's a delicious pasta dish with chunks of lobster, basil, and sun-dried tomatoes swimming in a rich, cheesy sauce.

"This is excellent," Hex says, his eyes on Cleo. She nods.

"I've always loved Francois' food. I can't understand why he's looking to sell. He can't be having money troubles."

"Don't let it ruin your meal. You can talk to him about it when we've finished," Hex prods. He glances around the table, likely looking for a way to distract Cleo. His eyes land on Pirate.

"I've accessed the network," Pirate says. "Want to see what I found?"

"Yes," Hex says as Pirate turns his laptop around so we can all see the screen. Olivia sits next to Pirate, so she has the best view. However, I can see enough to know he's pulled up the video feed for the hospital parking lot. I spot Olivia's car. I can see the silly cat ornament hanging down.

"Now watch," Pirate says. He hits the spacebar to start the paused black-and-white video. The lights on Olivia's car flash just before a man wearing scrubs, a mask, and a surgery cap comes into view. He opens the car door before reaching inside and popping the hood. Opening the hood, he leans inside before slamming the hood shut and walking out of view.

"I tried following him into the hospital but lost him inside."

Olivia nods. "He used my keys, didn't he? So, how did he get them? They were in my purse in the women's locker room."

"I'll study the video when we get back to the clubhouse. However, I counted dozens of staff members going in and out of the women's locker room before they tampered with her car until Olivia left."

"What about when I went to take my shower?" Olivia asks. "I had my phone with me all day. Someone could have taken it only when I was in the shower."

"Good thinking. Okay, I see you enter. Let's see. Yeah, eight people went in and out while you were in there. Do you recognize any of them?"

He plays the video for Olivia.

"Sylvia and Joyce both went in during that time. Could have been one of them."

"It could also be someone she doesn't know," I say. "If someone is working with these guys, they could be dressed in scrubs, too, but not be on staff."

"When we return to the clubhouse, I'll play around with the footage to see if I can get IDs on the other women. I'll also track the guy through the hospital. Might get a look at him without the gear or see who he interacts with," Pirate offers as he shuts his laptop and slides it into his messenger bag.

"Let's get back then," Hex says, pulling out his wallet.

"I want to use the restroom before we go," Cleo says, standing up. Delphine and Olivia follow her inside.

Hex digs out eight one hundred dollar bills and tosses them on the table to cover the tab and tip. We move to the lobby to wait for the women. I glance around the restaurant and see every table full of people enjoying their meal. We've moved past the lunch hour and are well into the dead period between lunch and dinner, yet the restaurant's packed. I spy several Tulane staff members, including the woman I had accosted while searching for Olivia the previous night. She's having a late lunch with someone I assume is a doctor, going by his expensive suit. Why did Francois approach us about investing in his restaurant? He seems to be doing well enough. I may recommend that we take Francois' offer seriously. If due diligence proves he's doing as well as I think, creating a partnership would be a no-brainer.

My phone pings. Toff. Shit.

"What?" I answer.

"Are you on your way?" he asks.

"No. Something came up. I'm still coming, but probably not until tomorrow."

When Toff doesn't respond, I check to see if we're still connected.

"Please come. The tribe needs your help, not just the medical shit. Something's going on. I don't know what to do about it."

"Like what?"

"I can't tell you everything over the phone. Some members of the tribe are having trouble with outsiders. I don't know how or why, but I know this relates to the clinic attack. I need you to come check things out. I could use a second opinion, especially from someone who understands how these people think."

I frown at his comment. "What does that mean? How the tribe thinks? You know them better than I do." I'd been off tribal land ever since the day after graduation. I may have gone back to visit, but I never spent more than a few hours with either Toff or our father. And I never spent time with anyone else within the tribe. That wasn't my life any longer. The Demon Dawgs are my family now.

"Not the tribe. There's a group of white men who are harassing our people. They've made threats against at least two of them. Maybe more. We don't know what the fuck they're after. I thought you could figure it out."

"Because I'm a criminal?"

"No, because you're part of a motorcycle club. So are they. I think. At least they ride around on bikes and wear the same type of vests you do."

"Kuttes," I correct him as I consider what he's telling me. "Do they have a club logo on the back?"

"I don't know. I haven't seen them. Just know they're bad news."

Suddenly, Hex and the others bolt down the hallway. What the fuck?

"Yeah, I'll be there tomorrow morning. Gotta go."

Chapter Ten: Olivia

We exit the patio and enter the restaurant. To our left is the hallway leading to the restrooms. In front of us is the hostess stand—Dr. Merkel and Joyce are waiting to be seated. I'd seen Joyce flirt shamelessly with the doctor, but I didn't realize she caught him. As I watch, Joyce pokes Merkel in the chest. He grabs her wrist hard enough to make her grimace. I move toward them just as the hostess leads them away.

Frowning, I catch up with Cleo and Delphine as Delphine pushes open the door to the women's restroom.

"Everything alright?" Cleo asks. "You look confused."

I chuckle. "Just a little. Saw Joyce having lunch with a doctor who works in our ward."

"Are nurses and doctors not allowed to date?" Delphine asks.

"No, they can date. Only they weren't acting like they were on a date. They seemed to be arguing."

"Sounds like a date to me," Delphine chuckles. "I swear whenever I drag Dixie to a nice restaurant, all he does is grumble."

"Hex is the same way," Cleo says before disappearing into a stall. Delphine ducks into the one next to hers.

I stand near the sink and wait for them to finish. Cleo comes out first. When she moves to the sink, I duck into her empty cubicle.

"I want to stop and say goodbye to Francois before we leave," Cleo says as I wash my hands.

"We'll come with you."

Cleo takes a right and continues down the hall until she stops in front of a door with Francois' name on it. She lifts her hand to knock but freezes.

"What's…?" I start, but she lifts her hand before shoving the door open.

I gasp at the scene before us. Two men hold Francois in his chair while a third punches him in the gut. The men look at us before Francois yells for us to run.

We don't. Instead, Delphine leans back into the hall and yells, "Dixie!"

The men release Francois before moving toward us. However, the sound of heavy boots coming closer makes them retreat. They climb out the open window and run off. When the last man turns his back on us, I can just make out the image of a large bird on the back of their kuttes.

Hex rushes in first, followed by the rest of his men. Dixie wraps his arms around Delphine while Lake grabs me.

"What's going on? What happened?" Hex demands.

"Those men were beating up Francois," Cleo explains. "Why?" The last she directs at Francois, who winces.

"They belong to some club extorting protection money from the businesses around here."

"For how long?" Hex asks.

"Six months. They're total assholes. Did you see the burnt remains of the bakery on the corner?"

Cleo nods. "Lydia's Sweets. I saw it. I thought she had an accident. Was it arson?"

Francois nods. "The cops said she burnt her bakery down for the insurance money. But I know she didn't. I saw those three bastards coming out of the place just before it blew. I think they turned on the gas. But they weren't alone; one had Lydia swung over his shoulder. I told the cops what I saw, but they didn't believe me. They accused me of taking money from her in exchange for providing her an alibi. The next day, those bastards came here and told me I'd be paying my and Lydia's share of the extortion money since I didn't mind my own business."

"They still have Lydia?" Hex asks.

Francois shrugs. "I don't know. She could be dead. If they have her, maybe she'd be better off dead."

"Who the fuck are they?" Abra demands.

"They were wearing kuttes," I tell him. "I couldn't make out the rockers, but the logo on the back had a bird on it."

"They're a motorcycle club?" Hex asks, looking at me before shifting his eyes to Abra.

"I'll put some feelers out. I haven't heard of another MC in this area. They could be pushing their way into our territory. They've been hassling you for six months? Did you see them before?"

"They introduced themselves seven months ago. Explained how things would work. At first, the amount they demanded wasn't worth the hassle of saying no. However, they increased the amount each month. Four months ago, Lydia told me she was going to the police. She'd lose her bakery if she kept paying them."

"That's when they burnt her bakery and kidnapped her?" Abra asks.

Francois nods. "After she spoke to the cops."

"Do you have them on video?" Pirate asks.

Francois perks up before pulling a laptop out of his bottom drawer. "The feed gets saved to our server, but I have access here." He logs into the computer before turning it around for Pirate.

"So, they're why you want us to invest? Were you planning on telling us what we'd be getting into if we took you up on your offer?" Hex asks, causing Francois to flinch as he nods.

"That was a mistake. I heard you discussing opening a restaurant, and I thought you could handle the threats. It was a gut reaction. I hadn't thought it through. It's why I told you to forget about it."

"What did they want today? A payoff?" Hex asks.

"They saw you enter the restaurant. They wanted to know if I told you about them. I told them I didn't, but they didn't believe me. With you running them off, they'll think I lied to them. They'll be back."

"Good. I want them to come back. We'll have a little surprise for them. Are there only three of them?"

"I've only seen those three."

"How many busboys you got working here?"

"Two."

"Okay, give them a paid vacation. Dixie, get Jack and Levi down here. They can fill in for the busboys. You don't have to pay them. They're prospects. They can protect you and the restaurant as well as keep their eyes open for those assholes."

Dixie steps away to make the call while Hex continues to tell Francois the plan.

"We'll dig into who the fuck these guys are. Once we have more information, we'll drive them out of New Orleans. In the meantime, just carry on with business, as usual. Tell them the Bratva has bought you out if they come back."

Francois' eyes widen. "The Bratva?"

"I have a connection." That is all Hex gives him. "That should keep them away. Tell them you've heard a rumor that the Bratva is taking over this neighborhood."

I see Hex's mind working as he formulates a plan. Glancing at Lake, he gives me a nod. "Levi will be fine. Those assholes won't know Levi and the other two are working for us. They'll be too busy looking for the Bratva to see us coming."

"But what about the Bratva? Won't they be upset you're using them as a smokescreen?"

Lake chuckles. "Hex's dad was the leader of the Bratva here. Maybe he still is. I don't know what Vladimir has done with him. Regardless, even if Vladimir is now in charge, they aren't in the city. Hex is counting on Vladimir telling his people to stay out of our business while he's out of town. We should be good for a few days. It will give us time to suss them out."

I nod as Hex finishes his instructions for Francois. "Did you get what you needed?" Hex asks Pirate, who nods as he closes the laptop. "Good. Let's ride."

We go outside just as Levi drives up in the club's SUV. Hex calls them over for their instructions.

The rest of us move toward the bikes. Lake hands me my helmet and then helps me fasten it. "I need to ask you a favor," he says when he finishes. "My brother called and wants me to come visit the tribe. They need medical help since their clinic shut down. I was hoping you'd go with me. You're off for the next four days, right?"

I nod. "Yeah, I can go. You want my help?"

"I could use it. I hope we can work out of the clinic instead of driving around to visit patients. However, Toff said someone ransacked the clinic. He thinks the supplies and the equipment are intact, but we'll know more when we arrive."

"What happened?"

"Don't know. Toff said they're having problems with a gang."

"Do you think it's tied to the men who attacked Francois?"

"I doubt it. The tribe lives two hours away."

Chapter Eleven: Lake

The following day, we set out early. Nora had coffee and breakfast sandwiches on bagels ready for us in the kitchen. As Nora bounces around the kitchen, Olivia and I eat sandwiches while chugging coffee. Olivia isn't much of a morning person, and I can't claim I am either. Nora, however, seems to be.

"What has made you so happy this morning?" Olivia asks her.

"The guys. They offered to set me up with a restaurant! Can you believe it? I'm terrified, but I'm also very excited. I dreamed of running a kitchen but figured it would take me years to earn enough money to invest in one."

"I didn't know Hex had already talked about it with you. That's great. I'm glad you're interested. We've all had your food and know your restaurant will be a success. It's a good investment for us," I tell her.

"I'll make sure you don't regret it," Nora assures me. "I have so many ideas. Cleo said she'd help me find a location and help with the planning and remodeling. I'm just so excited and grateful to you guys. You've done so much for me. Letting me live here and pay for my keep by practicing my cooking. I can't ever repay you."

"Make us lots of money, and we'll be happy." I grin at her.

"Have you thought about a theme?" Olivia asks.

"Not yet. Cleo, Delphine, and I are going to brainstorm later today. I have so many ideas that I keep jumping around. Hopefully, they can rein me in and help me decide. Unless you guys wanted something specific? Hex didn't say. Did you want the restaurant tied to the club? Like Zip's tattoo parlor, Marked by Demon? Should I call it Demon Diner? If so, I can come up with a diner menu." Nora's excitement diminishes as she considers her options.

"Hey, don't worry about that. Build the restaurant you want to build. We can figure out the name later. We don't have to tie the name to the club."

Nora smiles at me. "Okay, I'll stop freaking out. I'm just so excited. But I'm also afraid I'll let you down."

I take her hand and squeeze it. "You could never let us down. You aren't in this alone. We'll all pitch in and help. We want you to succeed. Okay?"

"Okay."

Olivia and I finish our breakfast and head outside. She goes to my bike, but I stop her.

"We have a two-hour ride ahead of us," I tell her. "You haven't ridden that long on the bike before. We can take the SUV. It'll be more comfortable."

She frowns and looks between the bike and the SUV. "I want to take the bike. I'll be okay. May have to walk it off once we get there, but I'm looking forward to a long ride."

"That's my girl," I tell her, placing her helmet on her head. We climb on my bike, and she wraps her arms around my waist. I take a minute to enjoy the feel of her wrapped around me—pure bliss.

To give Olivia a break, we stop at a gas station after an hour into our trip. I top off my tank while she walks off the stiffness.

"How are you doing? Sore?" I ask with a chuckle.

She smacks my arm. "Don't laugh at me."

"Do you want to use the restroom or get something to eat or drink before we keep going?"

"I'll use the restroom."

Taking her hand, I lead her inside the convenience store before going to the cashier to pay for my gas.

"We have surveillance cameras now," the kid behind the counter tells me.

I frown at him. "Okay, good for you. Why the fuck are you telling me?"

"I don't want any trouble. If you do anything, the owner will send the feed to the cops."

"I'm just getting gas. What makes you think I'll cause problems."

"Because you and your friends stopped here a week ago and stole from us. They beat up my friend who was working that day. Called him a bunch of names and sent him to the hospital."

"What the fuck? It wasn't my friends or me. What did these guys look like? Were they wearing kuttes?" I finger my kutte.

"Yeah, had a bald eagle on the back."

I turn and show him the Demon Dawgs logo. "Wasn't us," I repeat. "What did these guys look like?"

"I don't know. I didn't see them."

I grab a piece of paper and write down Pirate's number. "Call this guy. His name is Pirate. He's with my club. Tell him Lake told you to call. Tell him about these guys and when they were here."

The kid fingers the slip of paper before putting it in his pocket. "I won't get in trouble for this?"

"No, kid, we just want the information. We had a run-in with these guys yesterday. We want to find them and convince them to move on."

"Okay, I'll call."

Olivia comes out of the restroom as loud pipes echo outside. I step to the window and see three motorcycles riding past the gas station. Stepping outside, I rush to the street to look at them, but they're too far away.

Olivia's already at my bike with her helmet strapped.

"Were those the guys we saw yesterday at Francois' restaurant?"

"I don't know. I think so, but I didn't get a good look at them." I tell her about what the kid inside said about the attack on his coworker.

"We're over an hour away from Francois' restaurant. Is it normal for a motorcycle club to cover so much territory?"

I shrug. "Depends on the club and the area. Some clubs own entire towns and the surrounding area. New Orleans is big, so I wouldn't be surprised if more than one club wants in. Puma's club in Las Vegas owns all of Vegas, but he has another club in Vegas that they're allied with—the Shadow Bornes. The Demon Dawgs own San Diego because that's our mother chapter. Dante's father and grandfather made sure no other clubs took root. We're new to New Orleans. We don't have the numbers to take over the whole city. But so far, we've only seen three members of this club. If it's the same club and the same guys, they may be just starting out. Pirate and Abra are digging into them. We'll know more when they've gathered the info. Come on, let's go."

She climbs on behind me, and we continue our journey to the Terrebonne Parish, where our tribe lives and works. Unlike other tribes, the government doesn't recognize the United Houma Nation. Therefore, where the tribe lives isn't considered tribal land. We've been trying to gain recognition and territorial rights but haven't succeeded. Yet. The chief has made great strides toward this goal since he took over. Our people make a hard living in the bayou. They earn a living off fishing, trapping, shrimping, and crabbing. No one knows the bayou better than my people.

As we approach our land, I feel Olivia shifting behind me as she takes in the lush surroundings. Our neighborhoods don't have the typical suburban feel. Most everyone lives deep in the bayou, but that doesn't stop our tribe from maintaining close ties within the community. We have a few homes further inland for those who don't rely on the bayou for their livelihood. The main street houses the schools, library, general store, and a handful of homes. The tribe's chief lives in one of these homes.

He lives across the street from the public school and library. Growing up, I used to think he chose that location to keep an eye on all the kids. Later, I found out I was right. But he didn't do it for nefarious purposes. He watched the kids like any grandfather would watch his grandkids with pride and an eye for trouble. His house was large but not the largest on the street. That belonged to Dr. Solon. I knew from Toff that Dr. Solon hardly stayed in the house, not after the death of his wife. He has a daughter who was around Toff's age. I don't know what has happened to her. I hadn't seen her since she was sixteen before I joined the Army.

His door opens when I park in front of the chief's house. Toff comes outside to greet us, along with a young woman. She has the same long black hair, sculptured cheekbones, and copper skin tone enjoyed by most of the tribe. She looks familiar, but I can't place her. Besides, my attention immediately goes to the two men behind her, Coyote, the chief, and his brother, Crow.

Coyote is scowling at me as I swing off my bike before offering my hand to Olivia.

"What the fuck are you doing here?" Coyote snarls at me.

Olivia stumbles as she disembarks. Likely surprised by the venom in his tone. I steady her before taking her helmet, ignoring the chief as he approaches me. With my arm around Olivia, I turn to face the leader of our tribe. "Hello, Dad. Nice to see you, too."

Chapter Twelve: Olivia

The physical force of the chief's animosity toward Lake has me stumbling off the bike. I brace myself for the fall, but Lake's strong arms wrap around me and hold me steady. I expect him to stiffen at the man's words, but he seems unaffected. The older, angry man is muscular with broad shoulders and a commanding presence. I don't need to hear Lake's greeting to know these men are father and son. Looking at the chief is like looking into Lake's future. I can't say I'm not pleased to see he'll be just as hot when he's older.

The man next to the chief shares DNA but is a pale imitation—like a copy of a clone. However, the third man standing next to a beautiful woman must be Lake's younger brother.

"Hello, Dad. Nice to see you, too." Lake's tone is dismissive, but I can hear the tightness underlining his words.

"You can get back on that machine and get your ungrateful ass back to New Orleans."

"I will, once I've seen the patients Toff called me about," Lake says.

"Dad, we need Lake's help now that Dr. Sinclair is unavailable," Toff says.

"We don't need a medicine man. It's time your brother stops throwing his life away and accepts his role."

"I'm not having this conversation with you again. It isn't going to happen. I will never come back and take over as chief."

"You are my firstborn. It is your responsibility!"

"No. Your responsibility is to do what's best for the tribe. I'm not the best choice. You know it, I know it. Toff is the leader this tribe needs. Not me."

"Tradition…"

"Shouldn't become a detriment to the tribe. We have to evolve to survive. Our ancestors lived in thatched houses and made our clothes from the animals we hunted. You no longer live in a thatched house. You're wearing jeans instead of a breechcloth. Times change. When are you going to stop being so stubborn and recognize that Toff is the best fucking chief this tribe could hope to have?"

"I'm not saying Toff won't be an asset. He'll be your right-hand man, like Crow has been for me. It's time for you to come home."

Lake drops his head and takes a deep breath. "This is not my home. It hasn't been my home since I joined the Army. My home is in New Orleans with my club. They're my family now. My brothers."

"You think your wife will want to leave the tribe and live in New Orleans? Will you strip her of her family, too? Are you so selfish that you'd take her from everything she knows?"

I stiffen at his words. What does he mean? Lake's wife? Is Lake married? I shift away from Lake, but he pulls me closer to his side.

"That won't be a problem because I won't marry a woman from the tribe. I see my future, and that future includes Olivia. If she'll have me, she's the only woman for me." I glance up at Lake and take in the set of his jaw. He casts his eyes down to me and gives me a sheepish grin. "I know we haven't discussed marriage, but I can't deny how much I want a future with you."

"You can't marry her! She's not one of us. Annette is for you. She's our Medicine Woman. The tribe sent her to medical school. She's to stand at your side like your mother did for me. Your mother would be ashamed of how you've turned your back on us."

The gasp from the pretty and, until now, the silent woman standing next to Toff draws our attention. Coyote's face reddens as he sends her an apologetic look. "Annette…"

"Annette Solon?" Lake asks, leaving me and moving to the woman. She nods. He chuckles before lifting and swinging her around before putting her back on her feet. "I never would have recognized you. When was the last time we saw each other? You were what? Sixteen?"

"Yes," she says with a sweet smile. I feel a twinge of jealousy toward the lovely girl. Her long, straight hair is gorgeous. Light brown eyes stare at Lake out of a heart-shaped face. She's almost fragile in appearance with her slight body and short stature. I'm not a large woman, but I have curves—more curves than I want. Annette is like a perfect little doll.

I hear a growling noise and glance around. Thinking it's coming from Coyote, I glance at where he stood, but he's gone. My attention returns to Lake to see him watching his brother. He chuckles. "I see how it is. Don't worry, bro. I wasn't hitting on your woman. Just happy to see an old friend."

Lake backs up until he's next to me. He slides his arm around my waist and pulls me close again. I keep myself stiff, uncomfortable with everything that has transpired. However, Lake slips his thumb under my shirt to brush against my skin. His touch is intimate and conveys his message, mine.

"So, you're Dr. Annette Solon now?" Lake asks.

Annette shakes her head. "I just graduated from medical school. I still need to do my residency."

"Congratulations! You and Olvia can talk shop. She's training to be a nurse practitioner."

"Um, about what Coyote said. I didn't know he expected me...to you know...be..."

"Offered to me as a bribe?" Lake finishes for her.

Annette blushes and looks down. "Right. God, I'm so embarrassed."

"Don't," Lake and Toff say together.

"You have nothing to be embarrassed about," Toff continues.

"He's the one that should be embarrassed." Lake jerks his chin toward Coyote's front door. "Coyote is embarrassed. It's why he disappeared. He knows he has crossed the line but hides instead of saying he's sorry. He believes saying sorry makes one weak."

"He's only doing what's best for the tribe," Crow defends his brother.

"Is he? Because what's best for the tribe is Toff," Lake argues.

"But you are the firstborn. Leading the tribe is your legacy," Crow persists.

"The order of my birth isn't what makes a man a leader. It's something inside him. I don't have it, but Toff does. He has made himself into the person this tribe needs to succeed because that was his calling. At the same time, I've found my place with the Demon Dawgs. The United Huoma Nation will always be a part of me, but it is no longer my driving force."

Crow glances at me. "Because of her?"

"No. She's another reason, but I decided when I joined the army. I decided again when Hex started the Demon Dawgs. Olivia is the final piece. You know I'm right about Toff. As Coyote's second in command, you can help him accept the truth. Will you?"

Crow gives Lake an exasperated look but nods. "I'll see what I can do. Maybe this is for the best. Many in the tribe believe your club is responsible for our problems. "

"When did these problems start?" Lake asks after a long moment.

"Two weeks ago," Toff responds.

"I was in Ireland with my club for the last two weeks. We returned yesterday. It wasn't us, but I'll try to help you figure out who. However, this further proves why Coyote needs to stop forcing the issue. Why would the tribe follow a leader they believed terrorized them?"

Crow bows his head in agreement before leaving us.

"I didn't know your mother was your tribe's Medicine Woman. Is she why you became a medic in the Army?"

Lake chuckles. "Kind of. I hadn't signed on to be a medic. In BCT, I made a tincture out of marigolds to heal blisters. My mom knew everything there was to know about healing with herbs and plants. She taught me. I used that information to help my squad through training and deployment. When our medic got hurt, I took over."

"Is it a tradition for the chief and the Medicine Woman to marry?" I ask.

Lake frowns. "I don't think it's a rule or a tradition. My mom and dad did, but my father's mother wasn't the tribe's Medicine Woman."

"My grandmother was the Medicine Woman before your mother," Annette says. "She's why my dad went on to become a doctor. She's also why I followed in his footsteps. I found her old journal. She had a remedy for everything in that book. I saw myself solving all the world's illnesses with her knowledge." Annette laughs. "That hasn't happened, but I plan on using her cures in my practice. I want to bring back some of the simple remedies."

"That's a good idea," I tell her. "I wouldn't mind looking at it if you didn't mind sharing. Natural remedies often work just as well and with fewer side effects."

"I'd love to show it to you."

Toff glances at his watch. "We should get over to the clinic. Several men and women repaired and cleaned it so we could use it to see patients today."

"How much damage did they do?" Lake asks.

"Enough. We got lucky. Dr. Sinclair locked up the supplies and equipment in the X-ray room. The assholes tried to break through the wall but couldn't get inside. They broke chairs, cabinets, and the exam tables. We purchased two new exam tables from the hospital where Annette's father works. We also got some basic supplies from them. We should have everything you need."

Chapter Thirteen: Lake

The clinic is south of the town center, closer to those who require its services. Its location in the bayou, with only trees and wildlife as neighbors, makes it easy to understand how the men who attacked Dr. Sinclair and ransacked the building could do so without getting caught.

"How long before someone found Dr. Sinclair?" I ask Toff when we step out of the SUV.

"Two hours," Toff says, making me wince. "He's lucky he didn't bleed out. Doc was able to patch his wound. The assholes stole his cell phone and the office phone so he couldn't call for help."

Walking around the outside of the building, I see where someone tried to paint over something on the side wall. Stepping forward, I can make out a swastika. It will take several more coats of paint to cover it completely. But it tells me we're dealing with white supremacist trash. The current political climate has not only increased racism, but it has given the racists free reign to attack anyone different. While I continue my examination outside, Olivia and Annette go inside with Toff.

Behind the clinic is a small patch of muddy land, making spotting the motorcycle tracks easy.

I follow the tracks through the bayou and out the other side next to a road that leads into the main thoroughfare. Whoever these assholes are either scouted the area before the attack or someone told them about the shortcut.

Returning to the clinic, I went inside to assess the damage. Whoever cleaned up took more care to cover up the damage inside. Several coats of paint covered what I'm sure was more racially charged graffiti.

I toured the clinic when it first opened. I can see the damage they inflicted. The waiting room once had a wall of comfortable seats, but now it is empty except for two hard plastic chairs. The counter that once separated the waiting room from the rest of the clinic is gone. They gutted the first room, so I can imagine what they've done throughout.

"The walls had holes in them, and the graffiti was nasty," Annette explains.

"Do you have pictures of the damage?" I ask her.

"Toff does. We needed it for insurance."

"Good, I'll get him to send them to me. How much damage did these guys cause? Lose any equipment?"

"Just the furniture, the exam tables, and most of our basic supplies. Like tongue depressors, gauze, and bandages. They couldn't get to the medicine or the expensive equipment."

I follow Annette as she guides me through the clinic. I smell evidence of fresh paint in every room. The breakroom and the bathrooms have brand-new fixtures. Same for the exam rooms. The exam tables appear unused. At the end of the hallway, we stop at a closed door. Annette takes a keychain out of her pocket and unlocks the door. On the far side of the room sits various bulky equipment, including an X-ray machine, a CT scanner, and a mammography unit. Near the door is a locked medicine cabinet.

"When they built the clinic, they planned on adding the lead paneling to the walls surrounding this room to protect against radiation. However, Dr. Sinclair suggested adding steel paneling to keep out thieves. He knew the clinic was away from civilization, and we don't have any police presence."

"Smart move," I say. Looking through the glass on the medicine cabinet. "Do we have everything we'll need for the patients today?"

"We should. Most of those coming in only need vaccinations. Which we have." I follow Annette out of the room as we return to the breakroom to find Toff making coffee. "We might get someone coming in with an injury. If they do, we have antibiotics and pain medication. The only patients scheduled to come in are Muriel Oxbridge and Celeste Billiot. They're both pregnant and coming in for check-ups, including sonograms, which we can handle. Muriel is only four months in, but Celeste is due any day now. Dr. Sinclair was worried about her because the baby hadn't turned yet."

She chuckles when I grimace. "Looks like you and I will be handling them, Olivia."

"Can imagine you don't get much call to deliver babies in the Army or as a member of the Demon Dawgs," Olivia teases me.

"Hey, I've delivered a baby before. Once. We were in a village in the Middle East. The poor woman went into labor just as we were trying to evacuate the village. I'm proud to say she and the baby survived. However, I honestly can't remember much of the experience, what with bombs going off and bullets flying around us. As I recall, she did most of the work."

"That about sums up childbirth," Olivia says with a grin.

"We can take care of the mothers and the vaccinations. You can handle anyone else who comes in," Annette tells me.

I agree with their plan since it leaves me free to talk to the people Toff said were victims of harassment.

We hear the front door open and someone calling out. I step outside to see who has come in. In the waiting room is a man several years older than my father. He's holding an adorable little girl with big brown eyes. She's clutching a doll to her chest as she stares at me with suspicion. I guess her to be about five years old. Next to them is a young woman with the same dark eyes and hair as her daughter. She's holding a protective arm around her middle. I recognize the older man as Pieter Oxbridge. So, this means the young woman is either his wife or daughter-in-law. I remember Pieter's wife having died a few years back. Pieter has two sons. His oldest, Stefen, is my age, while his youngest, Manuel, is a few years younger than Toff.

"Pieter, good to see you," I say, holding my hand out to shake his.

"Lake. It's been too long." He shakes my hand before gesturing toward the young woman. "My daughter-in-law, Muriel. She's married to Stefen. And this little cutie is Marie. She's Stefen and Muriel's oldest."

I smile at Muriel before turning my attention to Marie. "Hello, Marie, who do you have there?"

Marie drops her head on Pieter's shoulder as she turns away from me. The older man jiggles his arm until the little girl turns her attention back to me. "Her name's Sutton. We don't want any shots."

"Marie's starting school in the fall. She needs her vaccines," Stefen explains, lowering his granddaughter to the ground.

"I see," I say as Olivia and Annette join us.

"I hear you're starting school soon. Are you excited?" Annette asks, taking the girl's hand and leading her away.

"They're in good hands," I assure Pieter, who watches them walk away as if he thinks he'll never see them again.

"We're keeping a close eye on both those girls," Pieter says. "We've had some trouble, and I'm not taking any chances."

"What kind of trouble?"

Pieter looks at Toff. "Did you tell him?"

"I told him outsiders are harassing some of our people, but I wanted him to hear you tell it. Joseph and Celeste are coming in later. I already told Joseph I want him to fill Lake in on what happened to him."

Pieter nods. "Two weeks ago, I heard several motorcycles pull up outside my house. I went out and found two young punks straddling their bikes. I told them to get off my land. They laughed at me and told me to return to where I came from. That spics weren't welcome. Before I could tell them off, the door opened behind me, and a third man dragged Muriel and Marie behind him."

"Fuck!" I explode, glaring at Toff for not telling me sooner. "What the fuck happened? Did they hurt them?"

Pieter shakes his head. "No, but only because they didn't get a chance. Stefen and Marcel came back and threatened to shoot them. The men hopped on their bikes and took off. Since then, Marcel's been staying home while Stefen does all the work. We're falling behind on our orders because he can't keep up, but they won't leave the girls and me home without backup. It's why I volunteered to bring the girls here today. That way, Marcel can help Stefen out."

"Did you tell my dad and Crow about this?" I ask.

"We did. The trouble is, no one knows where the assholes hang out or where they'll strike next. They attacked Joseph a few days after they came after me; then, they took out the clinic. They ride those fucking bikes so they're able to cover terrain cars can't."

I nod as I consider the situation. "Did you get a look at them? Do you think you'd recognize them again?"

"Fuck, yeah."

"You said they rode motorcycles. Did they have on kuttes?" When Pieter gives me a confused look, I thumb my kutte. "Like this? A leather or denim vest with a logo on the back?"

He nods slowly. "Yeah. They were all wearing denim vests. Had a bald eagle on the back."

"Anything else?"

Pieter shakes his head. "I didn't get a good look. I was too busy comforting Muriel and Marie. Maybe Marcel or Stefen saw more."

"I'll ask them. Okay, thanks, Pieter. Dad and Crow will probably hunt them down first, but I'll have my club look into it, too."

"I only came out of the house because I thought it was you and your club," Pieter admits. "You guys are the only bikers we know."

Chapter Fourteen: Olivia

Once we're in the exam room, Marie tells us, "I get to spend time with my friends. We also get to read and learn math. I can read a little and count to one hundred."

I help her onto the exam table while Annette preps. She swipes alcohol over the girl's arm while I distract her.

"That's amazing. I bet you'll be the smartest one there. Can you show me how well you count?" I ask her.

With Marie's focus on remembering her numbers, Annette makes quick work of the shot. Marie flinches when the needle enters, but she doesn't let the pain distract her.

Annette and I clap and praise the little girl while her mother beams proudly at her daughter.

"You were courageous, and you're brilliant," Annette says. "How about a lollipop?"

While Marie sucks on her candy, Annette and I set up the sonogram. Annette fiddles with the controls as I rub the lubricant on Muriel's bump.

"You're getting my mommy dirty," Marie complains.

"Don't worry, it comes off. We use this machine to see the baby. Are you excited about being an older sister?"

Marie shakes her head. "Babies cry too much."

"They do," Annette says as I rub the wand over Muriel's stomach.

"But that's why big sisters are so important. They get to help entertain the baby. I bet you'll be great at helping your mom care for the baby. Do you want a little sister or a little brother?"

"Sister," Marie firmly states. "Boys are loud and messy."

Marie's mouth drops open when the sound of the baby's heartbeat sounds throughout the room.

"What's that?" Marie whispers while her mother's eyes well up with tears.

"That's the sound of the baby's heartbeat," Annette says.

Marie's face breaks into a grin as she closes her eyes and listens.

"Everything looks good. You're 20 weeks?" Annette asks as Muriel nods. Muriel's eyes stay glued to the image on the screen.

"Want to know the sex, or are you waiting?"

"I want to know." She glances at her daughter, who is playing with her doll and not paying us any attention. "Is it a boy?"

Annette grins and nods. Muriel rolls her eyes. "Someone isn't going to be happy. However, my husband will be thrilled. He wanted a son."

"I'm getting a brother?" Marie screeches in disbelief.

Annette chuckles as I share a commiserating look with Muriel.

"Having a baby brother won't be so bad," I assure Marie. "I have a little brother. His name is Levi, and we're very close."

"Did you want a brother?"

"No, I didn't. So I can understand your disappointment. But one thing about having a brother: he never wanted to play with my dolls, but I loved to play with his trucks and other toys. So, I got to keep my toys and play with his toys. It was a win-win."

Marie snuggles her doll close as she considers my words. "I guess that would be okay."

Muriel climbs off the exam table and takes her daughter's hand. She thanks Annette and me. Marie turns to wave at us before turning back to her mother. "If I don't like him, we can send him back, right?"

"You have a brother?" Annette asks as we clean up. I nod. "What does he think of you dating a motorcycle club member?"

I chuckle. "Levi's the reason I met Lake. He was working for someone he thought was a businessman. It turned out he was part of the Russian mob. The asshole had kidnapped a woman and her two daughters. Levi helped them escape. The woman's son was the President of the Demon Dawgs. So, he took them to the Demon Dawgs clubhouse. Their President, Hex, offered Levi sanctuary for helping his mother and sisters escape. When the mobster came after me, Hex and the rest of the club rode in to rescue me."

"Brought lunch!" Toff calls out.

We join him and Lake in the breakroom, where two bags sit in the center of the table. Toff pulls several sandwiches out of one while Lake pulls chips, cans of soda, and water bottles out of the other.

I bite into my sandwich and moan in appreciation. I didn't realize how hungry I was. Looking up, I find Lake's heated gaze on me. That heat ignites a spark of desire and causes my breasts to become heavy with need. I can see he's just as tempted as I am to forego lunch and duck into the nearest exam room to feast on each other. To distract myself, I turn my attention to Annette.

"Where are you doing your residency?"

"Tulane Hospital. I'm starting in obstetrics."

"Really? That's where I work. What a coincidence," I say, glancing at Lake.

"What's it like?"

"That's a loaded question," I reply slowly. "It's a good hospital, but I've only worked there for a week. However, I have to warn you. Someone tampered with my car in the parking lot and then tried to kidnap me, and this isn't the first time it has happened."

"Excuse me?" Annette's eyes bug as Toff chokes on his sandwich. Lake slaps his brother on the back.

I tell her about the disappearance of the doctor and the nurse before giving her the details of my experience.

"If it wasn't for Lake and the other guys, they would have grabbed me."

"You don't know who they are? Are they doctors?"

"We don't know, but we're looking into it," Lake says. "Pirate is our tech guy. He's searching the camera feed to see if he can find images of the asshole without the disguise. Abra has feelers out for a white van with bullet holes in the doors and hood."

"Aren't you scared to go back there?" Annette asks.

"Yes, and no. Lake's making sure I don't drive to or from work alone. Now that I know someone can enter the women's locker room and get into my stuff, I'll bring another lock. I'll be extra careful not to find myself alone or vulnerable."

"I don't like the idea of you being there without protection," Toff tells Annette.

"Are you staying in an apartment?" Lake asks.

Annette nods. "Signed the lease yesterday. It's only two blocks from the hospital. I'd planned on walking…"

"No," Toff and Lake say together.

"Maybe you should consider completing your residency at a different hospital," Toff suggests.

Annette shakes her head. "I can't. I already committed to Tulane. I'll be careful. At least I know about the danger."

"Shit, you have your hands full," Toff says. "I shouldn't have dragged you into the problems here."

"No, I'm glad you did. We can handle it. Pieter mentioned seeing a bald eagle on the back of the biker's denim kuttes," Lake says.

"Like the men who attacked Francois?" I ask. "I don't understand. Do you think the same men who are extorting money from Francois and the other business owners are also coming out here to harass your tribe members? Why?"

"I don't know. Pieter mentioned seeing three men. The number of men we saw at Francois' and the same number of bikers the kid at the convenience store between here and New Orleans mentioned were causing trouble at the gas station. The club could be small, which would explain why Abra hasn't heard a thing about them from his contacts."

"If there are only three of them, they're busy," Toff says. Lake nods.

We finish eating just in time for our next patient. Toff shoos us out of the breakroom when we hear someone calling out from the waiting room. Lake, Annette, and I go out to find a man standing with his arm around a woman who looks like she's ready to go into labor at any second. From the grimace on her face, I think she might be.

"Celeste, you look uncomfortable," Annette asks, going immediately to Celeste's side after greeting Celeste and her husband Joseph. Joseph steps aside to speak with Lake while I introduce myself to Celeste.

I move to Celeste's other side when she doubles over. "Are you having labor pains?" I ask her.

"I wish. He's just very active. I'm so ready to be done. But I know Dr. Sinclair was worried because the baby hasn't turned yet."

"Let's get you comfortable and take a look," Annette says, wrapping her arm around Celeste's waist and leading her toward the exam room. I rush ahead and get ready for the second sonogram of the day.

"Let me help you," I offer as Annette and I help Celeste onto the exam table. Grabbing the lubricant, I lift her shirt before applying the gel to her swollen stomach.

Celeste grunts as I watch the baby's foot push up and out. "That's a good sign," I tell her. "Looks like the baby has turned."

"I hope so," Celeste hisses. "Oh shit!"

I glance down and see fluid flow over and off the table.

"Well, momma, it looks like your son wants out."

Annette and I help Celeste get comfortable.

"Can you let Joseph and Lake know what's happening?" Annette tells me.

Nodding, I rush to the door, but three men enter before I reach it. The first one waves his gun between the three of us while the other two take out zip ties. "Now, you're going to cooperate, or I'll gladly shove the gun up her cunt and kill them both."

Chapter Fifteen: Lake

Joseph stares after his wife with concern.

"She's in good hands," I assure him.

"I know Annette, but I don't know…"

"Olivia. She's my woman. She's an obstetrics nurse at Tulane Hospital in New Orleans. Like I said, Celeste and your baby are in good hands."

I remember Joseph from school. He was a year behind me, but we'd been friendly. Our community was small enough that all the kids knew each other. Some outsiders attended our school, but the tribe had the majority.

"Pieter was in here earlier with Muriel and Marie," I say, getting Joseph's attention. "He mentioned the men who threatened him and his family. He said they visited you. I was hoping you could tell me what happened."

Joseph runs his hand over his face. "Fuckers. Three of them came roaring onto our property when I was docking my boat. They came after me. After they punched and kicked me, they stopped long enough to lay out their threat. They told me they'd kill me and take my wife and child if I didn't clear out. Lucky for me, Stefen showed up, and they took off. Since then, Celeste has stayed with her folks whenever I go on the boat. I'm scared I'll come home and find my home destroyed or the assholes waiting for me."

"Did you tell the chief or Crow?"

"Spoke with Crow. He said they're looking into it. Crow and some others have been patrolling the community, but so far, no one knows where these assholes are hiding out. They show up, create havoc, and then disappear."

"Have they attacked others? Pieter thought it was just him and you. I found motorcycle tracks in the back. I think they may have caused the damage to the clinic."

"Yeah, Crow mentioned the tracks. They took out the clinic after they approached Pieter. Then they attacked me. I haven't heard of anyone else getting a visit from them, but they ride around the bayou and shoot off their guns. They're terrorizing our community."

"I hadn't heard about them causing havoc," I murmur. "Toff didn't mention it."

"This started happening two days ago. I heard them one night and ran into Baptiste, who mentioned it."

I consider why only the men have directly threatened the Oxbridge and the Billiot families and no one else. Maybe because Pieter and Joseph were alone? Three against one are good odds. Before I can ask any more questions, Toff stumbles into the room with his hand on the back of his head. When he pulls his hand free, blood coats his fingers.

"What the hell happened?" I ask, rushing forward.

"Guy jumped me when I was taking out the trash. Hit me over the head with something. I just woke up."

I force Toff into a chair so I can examine his head, but then a crash from down the hall has the three of us running into the almost empty exam room. Celeste is on the exam table, her feet inside the stirrups as she doubles up in pain. Someone zip-tied her ankles to the stirrups. I know neither Annette nor Olivia would have done that. Neither woman is in the room, but a surgical tray with gauze, scissors, and forceps lies on the floor.

"What happened?" I demand, only then realizing someone had wrapped gauze around Celeste's head to silence her.

"Baby," Joseph cries out, removing the gauze before kissing her forehead. "What happened?"

"Three men came into the room. One had a gun. They tied me up. They took Annette and Olivia. Same men. Same men who came to our house." Celeste gasps out. She screams as she clutches Joseph's hand.

"Fuck, you're having the baby. Okay. I've delivered a baby before. You're not alone in this. Toff, call for an ambulance. This baby isn't going to wait until they get here, but I want them on their way. Then, pick up the tray and the other stuff off the ground. I need you to find me sterile versions of everything that was on that tray."

"What about Annette and Olivia?"

I close my eyes and take a breath. "They have to be strong. This baby is coming. We need to focus on her and her mother."

"Okay, be right back." Toff takes off while I wheel a stool near the end of the exam table. I can see her dilated cervix and know she's close.

"How far apart are the contractions?" I ask.

"How the fuck should I know?" Celeste growls at me.

I chuckle. "Are they right on top of each other, or is there some time between them?"

"Fast, they're coming fast," she pants.

"Joseph, time the contractions. Help her breathe through them. I take it you attended the birthing classes and know what to do?"

Joseph nods.

"We don't have time to set up the monitors, so we're winging it. But you're young and healthy. Do you know if the baby turned?" I ask, remembering that this was something that had Dr. Sinclair concerned.

"Olivia said it turned. She saw the baby's foot high up on my stomach. My water broke before they did the sonogram." She screams through another contraction while Joseph lets her squeeze the hell out of his hand.

"Two minutes," Joseph says. I nod because I'd also been counting. This baby is about to make its appearance.

I'm about to yell for Toff when he comes rushing in with the requested supplies. He places them on the table and rolls them over to me. "What else do you need?"

"Fill that tub with warm water, then find me a baby blanket and several washcloths. When you've done that, call Crow and get everyone out there looking for those assholes and the women. Then call Hex. Tell him what happened. What about the ambulance?"

"They're forty-five minutes out, but they're on their way. They have a doctor you can call if you need her to walk you through the birth or have complications."

"I've done this before, in worse circumstances, but that's good. Now, little mama, let's bring your baby into the world. Shall we?"

Several minutes later, I'm holding a screaming baby in my hands.

"Congratulations, you have a son."

Joseph clasps Celeste's hand as he stares in awe at the bundle in my hands.

"He's so small," Joseph whispers as if raising his voice would make the infant disappear.

"I'm going to clean him off, and then I need you to cut the umbilical cord."

"What?" Joseph stammers, clutching Celeste's hands so tight she squeaks. "Sorry, baby."

"Come over here and pick up the scissors. Let me clamp the cord first." I attach one clamp about three inches from the baby's stomach and place the second clamp nearer to Celeste.

"Just cut there, on this side of the clamp," I instruct Joseph. With shaking hands, he completes the task. I dry the stump before instructing Joseph on how to diaper his son while leaving the stump of the cord exposed. He leaves to follow my instructions while I focus on helping Celeste through the afterbirth.

Joseph returns to place the baby against Celeste's chest. Mother and son are both exhausted. Joseph is right there with them.

I step out of the room to find Toff. He's pacing the waiting room with the phone to his ear. He has a map of the community laid out in front of him. I step over to find he'd drawn grids across the map. He'd scribbled a name into each grid box. Two of the grids contain large Xs. He marks another grid with an X as I watch. "Keep me posted." Ending the call, he looks at me. "I've mobilized the tribe. They're searching for the girls. We can stay here and monitor the progress or head out and join the search."

"Leave me your phone, and I'll stay here and monitor," Joseph offers. "Celeste is resting with the baby. She wants me to help you find Annette and Olivia."

"Thanks, man," I tell him, clasping him on the shoulder. As I turn away, I remember what Celeste said.

I rush into the exam room. Celeste, who is breastfeeding her son, looks up. "Did you find them?"

"No, we're still looking. Thank you for letting Joseph help us. I have a question for you. You said they were the same men who attacked Joseph. How do you know? Did you see their faces?"

"No, I saw what they were wearing. They had on denim vests with a bald eagle on the back. I think they're part of a motorcycle gang. The bald eagle was clutching two flags in its talons. One was the Confederate Flag, and the other was a Swastika. At the top was the word 'Third,' but that's all I could see."

"Thank you, that helps. You rest and take care of your son."

I return to the waiting room to find Toff giving Joseph last-minute instructions.

"You have my phone. Lake's number is in there. Everyone knows to call my number to check in as they finish their sweep of their assigned areas. The areas without a name are the ones that still need someone assigned to search."

I'm studying the map and see two grids without names. They're on the outskirts of the community. "We'll take these two," I tell Joseph. When he leans over to write in our names, I tug on Toff's arm and propel him towards the door.

"Who lives out where we're going?"

"No one. That's why I had assigned no one to search the area yet. There's only one homestead out there. It used to belong to Running Bear. He died last summer, and it's sat abandoned since."

I share a look with Toff. Our first stop is Running Bear's former cabin. As Toff drives, I text Pirate with the information Celeste gave me.

Chapter Sixteen: Olivia

"Here's what's going to happen. You two are coming with us. Don't make a fucking sound. I'll gladly shoot the bitch and her spawn. Take these and tie her to the bed." He hands us each a zip tie. We reluctantly attach her ankles to the stirrups. When we finish, he shoves a roll of gauze into my hand. "Gag her." I wrap the gauze around her mouth, staring into her tear-filled eyes. "Tighter, or I'll do it and make it hurt." With an apology, I tighten the gag.

"Good enough. Now, let's get moving. Out the back and don't make a fucking sound."

Annette and I glance at each other before following them outside. I see Annette slide a scalpel into her jeans and wish I could mimic her action. Celeste whimpers as we leave. The leader stays inside with Celeste while the others drag us through the swamp. I'm terrified for Celeste. What if the asshole who stayed behind hurts her? Or what if he kills her and her child? I don't know whether to be relieved or concerned when he catches up to us a few minutes later. I didn't hear the sound of a shot, so I'm hopeful he left Celeste alive. After several minutes, we break into a small clearing containing three motorcycles.

Two hop on their bikes while the third waves the gun at us. "Get on the back."

We both balk, but the one with the gun steps up to Annette and places the barrel between her eyes. I scramble onto the back of the bike nearest me. The driver grabs my wrists and pulls them to the front. He zip-ties my wrists together. I glance over to see Annette on the second bike, with her wrists also tied.

"Don't think about making them crash. I'll be behind you. I'll shoot you if I have to."

The man I'm strapped to smells like he has a religious aversion to soap. I try shifting away from him to get some fresh air. He reaches up and yanks my arms forward again so I'm plastered against his back. The man who threatened us rides up next to me and aims the gun at me. I don't think he'll shoot. He'd risk his friend, but I take heed of the warning. Luckily, the drive is quick, and we pull behind a cabin.

The leader parks far enough ahead that I can make out the logo on his kutte. A bald eagle with his wings pulled wide. In each talon is a flag. The flag on the left is the Confederate flag, while the other is a German flag displaying the Swastika. The assholes stole America's icon and defiled it with the flags of our enemies. Fuckers. The words 'Third Reich' stretch over the emblem, but the bottom rocker is missing. I'm confident this is the same emblem the assholes at the restaurant had on their backs. So, the gang extorting money in New Orleans are the ones harassing Lake's people. However, these men aren't the same ones who entered the restaurant. So, the gang has at least six members—maybe more. We need to get away from these men so I can tell Lake.

Once they've cut the zip ties, our drivers grab our arms and yank us inside. The third man follows with his gun still out. We can't escape. They march us through the house and into the kitchen. However, they lead us into a cellar before I can look around. The cellar lacks a window, so the only light comes from the open door at the top of the stairs.

I hear Annette sniffle next to me. I'm too pissed to cry.

"What do you want with us?" I demand.

They ignore me.

"You've signed your death warrants. The men we were with are going to come looking for us, and when they find us, you're dead."

The man with the gun smirks at us, but the one I rode behind snorts. "Fucking injuns? I hope they come. I'm ready for some target practice. Riding around in circles like a bunch of dumb fucks. We can pick them off one by one. Stupid motherfuckers."

His accent tells me he's from the Deep South, likely Alabama. I can picture him yelling 'yee haw' as he hops onto his motorcycle. He's wearing dirty jeans and a faded shirt with the wording 'Real Men

Shoot Their Load.' Classy.

Annette snorts with derision. "Those old movies were shit. Only an idiot would believe them. So, I'm not surprised you do."

He swings his arm back to backhand her, but the leader snaps at him.

"Leave it. Our friend wants them without marks. I'm not risking the payday because you're a moron."

I share a look with Annette. Someone wants us? Why?

"Who wants us? Who are you working for?"

"You'll find out soon enough. In the meantime, you're just a distraction. Your disappearance will keep those assholes busy."

With those words, they climb the stairs, slamming the door shut behind them. I hear the lock slide into place. We're trapped in the dark.

"We need to get out of these zip ties," Annette says, moving next to me. "See if you can get the scalpel in my pocket."

My eyes have adjusted to the darkness so I can make out shapes. Finding Annette, I feel for the scalpel in her pocket. Sliding my fingers in, I carefully remove it.

"Pull your wrists apart as wide as you can," I instruct her. She does, which gives me just an inch to work with. Taking great care, I slide the scalpel into the gap before cutting the ties. I can't risk knicking her with the scalpel. The consequences are too dire. Once I cut her ties, she cuts mine. We can at least move around. Plus, we have a weapon. I'm hoping we can find another.

"I know where we are," Annette says, putting the scalpel back in her pocket.

"Where?"

"This is Running Bear's home. He died a few months ago. His kids moved away and left this place abandoned."

"I don't suppose Running Bear built a secret entrance to his cellar, by any chance?" I ask in jest.

"Maybe. Sometimes, cellars often have more than one entrance. Let's look around and see if we can find one."

We each move in different directions to start our search. I can't see past my face, so I use my hands. Not that I expect to find a hidden door, but at least we're doing something other than worrying about the men coming back. Or worse, the men leaving us here.

"Dammit," Annette curses from across the room.

"What happened?"

"I tripped over these logs. Wait. This is an entire stack of logs."

"I don't think we should start a fire down here," I chastise her, even though I feel the room's chill.

"I wasn't recommending we start one, but this stack of wood is not near the door. I don't see Running Bear hauling this wood down those steps and storing the wood this far from the door. He probably has a trap door above this pile that he used to drop the wood from outside. We need to move this wood out of the way."

"I have an idea." After several trips, we have created a barrier that will delay our captors from reaching us. We've stacked the logs five layers deep. They can't push open the door without alerting us and exerting some strength. Lucky for us, none of the men were muscular. We've also worked up a sweat, so we no longer feel the chill.

"Okay, we need to search the top of the wall and the ceiling," Annette instructs.

We begin our search again. This time, I'm the one who makes a discovery. "I think I feel something. Feels like a slit in the wall." Whatever it is, it sits high up on the wall.

We shift a few logs to build a platform on which to stand. When we both find hinges, we hit pay dirt.

"I have the handle. Here, help me pull," Annette says. I locate her hands, and we both pull on the metal ring. The trap door pops open. "Good. Let's get out of here. I'll help you up, and then you can help me. Once we're free, head for the bayou. I can lead us through it."

Since I'm several inches taller than Annette, I quickly pull myself up through the opening. It's a tight fit, but I manage. Turning, I reach down and grasp hold of Annette's wrists. That's when we hear the men attempt to open the door. They cuss and throw themselves at it when they can't shove it open. Annette scrambles up, using my body as a ladder. I'm helping her through when I hear a gun go off. Pain rips across my scalp as we tumble backward onto the ground.

"Move!" Annette hisses. We make a beeline for the thick foliage. The fear of a bullet in my back gives me speed.

Chapter Seventeen: Lake

The cabin is still habitable but showing apparent signs of neglect. Whoever built it fought a raging battle against the surrounding bayou, carving out the land to construct a home, but nature was taking it back. Kudzu and trumpet vine were sneaking toward the cabin like a predator stalking its prey. Alligator grass followed in its wake, ready to smother what remained of a vegetable garden. The numerous tracks from the road to the house proved we weren't the first visitors. Several motorcycles had crossed through the overgrowth. Many of the tracks were old, but I spotted recent ones. This is the place. I'm sure of it.

Not taking any chances, I direct Toff to continue past and park out of sight.

"I'll check it out. You wait here," I tell Toff. He nods as I slide out and silently shut the door. Keeping to the trees, I go through the overgrown foliage until I can see the back of the cabin. Three motorcycles sit in the back nearest the door. Hoping three motorcycles mean only three men inside, I return to the SUV.

"I think this is the place. Three motorcycles. They're hiding out here if they're the guys who took the girls. I'm going in," I tell him, palming my gun. I pull up my pant leg to reveal a second gun. "You armed? If not…"

"I'm armed," Toff says, opening the glove box and taking out a Glock. "I called Joseph. He's sending some guys our way."

"I'm not waiting. If they get spooked, they'll book it. We can't take a chance on them harming the women. So, let's go. We can take them."

Using the foliage as cover, we move until the cabin comes into view. The bikes are still there. The side facing us has a single window, but it's high up on the wall, so it's likely a bathroom. We run forward and plaster our backs against the wall.

"You go through the back, and I'll come in through the front." Toff nods, moving into position, while I slide against the wall toward the front door. Reaching the corner, I turn to watch Toff's progress. He snaps his head around the corner before snapping it back. But instead of giving me a nod, I get a frantic wave. I'm uncertain about what he's trying to tell me, but the echoes of revving engines clue me in. Fuck!

Three motorcycles fly around the corner, speeding past Toff. The one in the lead spots him, but he is too late to take a shot. However, he sees me and shoots. He misses, but having to drop to the ground costs me my chance. I return fire, but they're far enough away that I doubt I hit anything. However, I did see one wobble before righting himself. So, who knows? Maybe I winged one. The road they're on will take them to Highway 90. Taking out my phone, I call Hex.

"Did you find them?"

"Not yet. We found where they took the girls, though. Toff and I are about to go inside. The fuckers just left on bikes; the three of them are headed toward 90. You might pass them. I might have winged one."

"We'll be on the lookout for them."

I tell him about the gas station and convenience store where Olivia and I stopped. If I hit one, they may stop there to patch up the wound before continuing if their goal is New Orleans. "Did Pirate fill you in on their club logo?"

"White supremacists," Hez spits. "Fucking hate those neo-Nazi assholes. It sounds like the same guys at Francois' restaurant. What the fuck is the connection between the restaurant and your people?"

"No fucking clue," I say, ending the call as Toff joins me.

"Did they have the girls?"

I shake my head. "No. Each biker was solo. You go through the back as planned. I'll go through the front. The place may not be empty, so keep your head down."

Entering through the front, I find myself in a small hallway. There's an open door to my left and another to my right. Standing still, I let my senses explore the space. I can hear Toff moving at the back but no other sounds. A quick look to the right reveals what could either be a bedroom or a dining room. Considering there is a mattress on the floor next to a table, I concede it could be both. There is a second door at the back of the room. Before heading for it, I clear the room on the left. It's empty except for two mattresses and trash. Broken glass in the corner tells me the assholes squatting here would toss their empty beer bottles against the wall. Pigs.

There is a door off this room, too, but a glance reveals it's a bathroom. It was just as disgusting as I expected. The room smells as if no one bothered to hit the toilet.

I move back into the other room and go through the door into the kitchen, where I find Toff.

"Anything?" I ask.

"Just a fuck ton of garbage. Although, I found this." He hands me a pamphlet filled with racist garbage and touting the need to keep American bloodlines pure. There are ample images of swastikas alongside the confederate flag. Several paragraphs on how the filth from other nations has tainted American soil. On the back is a picture of a bald eagle in attack mode. Clasped in its talons are the confederate flag and, in the other, the flag of Nazi Germany. Under the image is the phrase, 'Keepers of the Third Reich,' with an address in Nevada. I fold the brochure and stick it in my kutte.

"They aren't here," Toff says, slamming his fist into the wall.

The cabin has only a handful of rooms. We've explored each one. If the girls aren't here, then where the fuck could they be? "Let's look again. We must have missed something. Is there a cellar or an attic?"

"There should be a cellar," Toff says. We find it behind the refrigerator. The assholes likely moved the appliance to the block off the entrance. Maybe they're hoping we'd leave so they can return and grab the girls. Feeling like we're sitting ducks, I urge Toff to hurry.

"I can't budge the door," Toff grunts.

"Let me try," I offer as we switch places. Heaving myself against the door, I can only shift it two inches. It's enough for Toff to shine the flashlight from his phone.

"Do you see anything?" I ask him.

"It's the cellar. I can't tell what's blocking the door."

"Olivia! Annette!" I call out. "Are you down there?"

We get silence in return.

"Let's try opening the door again," I suggest. We get in position and shove. The door moves another two inches—just enough for Toff to push his head through.

"Fucking logs. Someone has stacked logs against the door. But I can see an opening on the far wall. We might get in through there. Let's go."

We hustle outside and search the back of the house until we find an opening. I drop to the ground and peer inside the dark hole. Logs litter the cellar floor, and I can see a pile of logs at the top of the stairs. Grinning at their cleverness, I back out. However, my grin slips when I spot the small puddle of blood.

"I found their tracks," Toff calls out. "They're headed into the bayou."

"We need to go after them. One of them is bleeding."

"We should be able to track them, then," Toff says, looking at me. I know what he's thinking. If we can track them, so can the predators. The girls may not be running from their kidnappers now, but they aren't safe. Not yet.

"We need flashlights."

"I have a couple in the SUV. I'll be right back." Toff returns a few minutes later with a pair of Maglites. He hands me one as he switches on the other. We're able to track them easily. We have grown up learning to track animals from an early age. Tracking requires patience, something I've never had difficulty summoning until now. I barely stop running through the overgrowth and calling out for Olivia. Knowing she's out there and possibly hurt guts me.

We hear the occasional splash, reminding us that we aren't alone out here—that the girls aren't the only ones the predators are stalking. However, in our case, we're armed. The girls aren't.

"Don't worry, Annette knows this area. She's leading Olivia to safety through the narrowest part of the bayou. There is a road on the other side."

His confidence builds up my hope. But that shatters with their screams.

Chapter Eighteen: Olivia

Pain sears through me as I clutch at my scalp. I don't have to see the blood to know I'm bleeding. My fingers are sticky with it. The bullet must have grazed me. The thing about head wounds is they bleed—a lot.

"Annette," I call out as I follow her through the swamp. "That bullet grazed me. I'm bleeding."

"Shit. Can you continue?"

"Yes, but I need to stop the bleeding." Ripping my shirt, I press the fabric against the wound. It won't be enough to staunch the blood completely, but hopefully, it will stop it from dripping and leaving a trail.

"Lean against this tree. I'm going to look for some moss."

Did she say moss? Before I can ask, she's gone.

A few minutes later, she returns with her hands full of plants.

"What are you going to do with that?" I ask her.

"It's Spanish Moss. Put it over the wound. It won't stop the bleeding completely, but it will soak up some of the blood. It will also keep the wound clean."

As she suggests, I press the moss to the wound and nod for her to keep going.

"We have to keep to the ground and stay away from the water," Annette instructs me. "Also, watch the trees. That's where the snakes hide. They'll drop on you if you're not paying attention."

I stumble as she describes all the various animals out here that want to kill us. Maybe we'd be better off going back to the cabin. But remembering the looks in their eyes, I'm sure that I'd prefer to be killed quickly by something out here than face the nightmare of what they had in store for us. As I follow Annette, I realize that if I were out here alone, I'd be a goner. But with her, I have a chance.

We stay on solid ground, but the occasional splash of water reminds me we aren't alone. I expect an alligator to leap out of the water and grab me. Of course, I also expect the men to catch up to us. I'm getting dizzy with my head on a constant swivel. Every so often, Annette snags more moss and hands it to me. She takes the used moss and drops it into the water. I guess so we don't leave a trail.

"Won't that bring the alligators?" I ask Annette.

"They aren't sharks," Annette tells me, which makes me feel better until she continues. "They can scent blood out of the water."

The sky continues to darken. I don't know how Annette finds her way through the swamp with so little light. I want to ask, but I'm afraid to do so. So far, none of her explanations have brought me comfort.

I'm exhausted. The hauling of the logs, the blood loss, and the humidity combine to make me want to curl up and sleep. But I know we can't stop until we get out of this blasted swamp.

When Annette stops walking, I'm so lost in my thoughts that I almost bump into her. I'm about to question her, but then I hear a noise that stops my heart. Something, or someone, is crashing through the foliage and coming straight at us. My first thought is that the assholes found us, but then I hear loud snorts and know whatever we're facing isn't human.

"Shit, boars, climb the tree," Annette orders, pushing me toward the nearest cypress tree. She pushes me up onto the trunk before scrambling up behind me. We're only three feet off the ground when two enormous beasts burst through the undergrowth and run toward us. I can't stop myself from screaming as they circle the tree trunk. Annette doesn't have to push me to climb higher. I swear they grow larger as they get closer. Annette's foot is only inches away from their snouts.

"Can you reach the next limb?" Annette asks.

I glance up and measure the distance. I can't reach it from where I'm sitting. But if I can get on my knees or stand, I might be able to close the distance. Not wanting to fail Annette, I shift until my knees are under me. Glancing down, I see the boar make a jump that brings him much too close to her. The limb I'm on is on the thin side, but I get my foot planted in front of my knee. Using my arms to maintain my balance, I slowly rise and grab hold of the limb above me. Pulling myself up, I wrap my entire body around it. Relief pours through me when Annette takes the spot I vacated. We're both out of reach of the frustrated boars. I don't know how long we can hold on with the pair circle below us. Our strength will give it out long before they tire of waiting.

"How are you doing?" Annette asks. "How is your head?"

"I'm okay enough for now." I lean my cheek against the limb while I use my right hand to check the wound. I feel the stickiness of congealing blood. "I think I stopped bleeding."

"Good. I'm hoping they give up soon. Shit. Do you hear that?"

Fuck! What now? I listen hard but only hear the boars huffing and puffing below us. But then I hear large bodies crashing through the foliage, preceded by shouting. Shots scare the boars off before two dark shapes pass below us. Seeing Lake and Toff almost causes me to lose my grip on the limb.

Toff helps Annette climb down, and Lake comes to assist me. I cling to him as he holds me.

"Are you alright?" Lake hoarsely whispers as I lose myself in the safety of his arms.

"I am now."

"Which one of you is bleeding?" Lake asks.

"Me. But I think it's stopped."

"Let me see," Lake says. He shines the flashlight on my wound. "Still oozing a little blood. I need to examine it, but somewhere else. How did it happen?"

"Those bastards shot at us when they saw us escaping. The bullet grazed me. I don't think they meant to hit either of us. They were probably just trying to scare us."

Lake's jaw clenches as he fists and unfists his hands.

"They might be looking for us," Annette says. "We should get out of here before they come or the boars return."

"The fuckers who grabbed you took off. But, yeah, we should get out of here," Toff agrees.

Lake takes my hand while Toff takes Annette's.

Toff takes the lead, and soon, we're out of the swamp and standing next to a road. A short distance away sits a truck with a man standing beside it.

"You found them? Good," he says, moving to open the door to the backseat.

"Baptiste?" Lake greets him. "How did you know where to find us?"

"Joseph said you were going to Running Bear's cabin. I went there, but couldn't find you. I saw your SUV and the tracks leading into the bayou. So, I figured you were coming through this way. Glad to see I was right. Hop in, and I'll take you to your car."

Lake squishes his bulky frame into the back with Annette and me. Toff stands outside with the phone pressed to his ear. When he ends the call, he climbs into the passenger seat and turns to face Lake.

"I told Joseph we found them and to call off the search. He's sending a couple of guys over to watch Running Bear's place to see if they return."

"How is Celeste? Did she have her baby?" Annette asks.

"She did. Lake helped her deliver her son. It was fucking awesome to watch him work." Toff grins at his brother. But I feel Lake tense up next to me.

I lean against Lake and stroke my thumb against his hand. "You did the right thing. Helping Celeste before coming after us."

Lake kisses the top of my head. "I know, but it doesn't change how wrong it felt."

"We need to update the chief," Toff interrupts us.

"Update him about what?" Baptiste asks.

"The men who kidnapped Olivia and Annette. They're part of a neo-Nazi club," Lake explains.

"I saw the back of their kuttes," I chime in. "They had the words 'Third Reich' over the emblem of an eagle holding two flags."

"Like this?" Lake asks, pulling something out of his kutte and handing it to me. I recognize the emblem immediately.

"Yes. But this says their base is in Nevada. Why are they here?"

"I don't know. Also, I don't know why they're harassing our tribe and a bunch of business owners in New Orleans. I'm hoping Abra and Pirate can gather more information about them."

"Abra and Pirate?" Baptiste asks.

"My brothers in the Demon Dawgs. I sent them the information I found, and they're out looking for the bastards who took Annette and Olivia."

"They're coming here?" Baptiste asks.

"They're headed this way."

"Olivia needs to go to the hospital," Lake states.

"What about updating the chief? Don't you need to go there first?" I ask Lake. "I'm not showing any signs of a concussion, only a slight headache. Let's go back to the chief's house. I'd like to shower and change my clothes before we go to the hospital. I have a pretty good idea of how long we'll be sitting in the waiting room, and I'd rather do it in clean clothes."

Lake smirks at me. "Okay, we'll update the chief first. Besides, I can clean and bandage the wound before we go."

Baptiste pulls up next to Toff's SUV. We pile out of his truck and climb into the roomier vehicle. Rather than sitting up front with Toff, Lake climbs in behind me.

When we pull up to Coyote's house, I glance at the door and frown. "Does your dad always leave his door open?"

Chapter Nineteen: Lake

Olivia's statement has all of us turning our attention to the house. As chief, my father's door is always open, but figuratively, not literally. But there it was, wide open. My gut churns as I leap out of the SUV, stopping only long enough to shout at my brother. "Stay in the SUV, protect the women."

Pulling out my gun, I step inside. Pausing to listen, I hear someone coming in through the back door. Turning in that direction, I expect to find Toff, but instead, it's Crow.

"What's going on? Why are you carrying a gun?"

"Dad's door was open. Any reason why he might do that?"

Crow shrugs. "I don't know. Maybe he didn't shut it all the way, and it blew open?"

"Or maybe someone was in a rush to get the hell out," I say, nodding toward a mess of papers lying outside Dad's office. Pushing Crow to stay behind me, I stand at the door and scan the room. Papers cover every surface. It looks like a copier exploded. Stepping into the room, I take in the damage. The bookshelf that once held all the tribal records for generations is now empty. Their contents are tossed haphazardly around, along with the contents of several file cabinets. Every drawer in my father's desk lies upended on the floor, their contents dumped. Someone wanted to create a mess, or they were looking for something. Not seeing my father, I turn to Crow. "We need to check his room and search the house. Toff has a gun so that you can arm yourself. I don't think whoever did this is still here, but don't take any chances." Crow nods and jogs outside.

Before I can back out of the room, I hear a moan that draws me to the bathroom connected to his office. The door's partially ajar, so I push it open, only to find it blocked. Sticking my head through, I spot my father on the ground. He's on his back, blood pooling at his side and soaking his shirt—too much blood. Kneeling, I feel for his pulse. I let out my breath when I felt a faint pulse.

"Lake," my father grunts. Lifting his hand, he grasps mine. I think he's looking for comfort, but I feel him push something hard into my hand. A USB drive. "Don't let him..." But he loses consciousness before he can finish.

"Don't let who?" I mutter, shoving the USB drive into my pocket as I pull out my phone to call for an ambulance.

"Lake?" Crow calls from the door. I step back into the office.

"I found Dad. He's hurt. I called for an ambulance. Get Annette and Olivia. They can treat him until it arrives. Go," I bark the order when Crow approaches me instead of doing as I asked. Dad needs help.

Olivia and Annette rush in and look at me. I nod at the bathroom door and watch them disappear inside. Toff comes in and looks around the room.

"Stay with the girls. I'm going to check the rest of the house. The ambulance should be on its way. The hospital is re-routing the one we ordered for Celeste."

"How is he?"

"Alive, and I hope to keep him that way," I say before making the rounds around the house. I check every room except one. My old bedroom is locked up. Bypassing it, I verify that no one else is in the house. No other rooms show the same level of destruction as the office. So either the person who attacked my father found what he wanted, or he got spooked before he could extend his search. When the ambulance pulls up, I return to the office in time to see the EMTs rush in, pushing a gurney.

I stand in the hallway to stay out of their way. Toff joins me. "Where's Crow?" I ask him.

He shrugs. "He took off after he told us what was going on. I don't know where he went."

Frowning, I don't have time to think about Crow because the EMTs are wheeling out our father. I study the frail man on the gurney as he passes under the hallway light. He's pale, his face slack. I've never seen my father sick, so his appearance jolts me. I must have made a noise because Toff clasps me on the shoulder, and Olivia wraps her arms around me. I squeeze her tight before remembering that she's injured, too.

"Maybe you should go with them. Get your head looked at," I suggest.

"I don't want to get in the way. It's better if they focus on your dad. I feel fine. We can go to the hospital, and I'll check myself into the ER."

"Want to run next door and wash up first?" Annette asks Olivia, who nods gratefully. They leave Toff and me in the hallway. We're staring into the office, both of us lost in our thoughts.

"I've called the cops. They're on their way," Crow says, returning to the house. "I can talk to them if you two want to go to the hospital."

"Where did you go?" I ask him.

"To call the police and to call the elders to let them know what happened. We need you to step up while Coyote is out of commission," Crow says.

I grimace, knowing he's right. While I want to insist that Toff take my place, I know it won't fly with the elders. We'd be bucking tradition; the tribe needs stability, not more upheaval. I glance at Toff.

"You have to. We need to call a meeting and tell everyone what happened and what we know. Our tribe is under attack. Everyone expects you to take over. I know it isn't what you want."

"But it's what I must do, at least for the interim. While you wait for the cops to arrive, contact the elders again and tell them I need to meet with them," I direct Crow. "I don't know how long we'll be at the hospital, so make it for sometime tomorrow morning."

He steps away to make the call while I run my hand through my hair in a failed attempt to calm my nerves. Taking over as chief of the tribe was a role I've avoided ever since Dad laid out the plan when I turned twelve. That day, he explained every detail of my life as if it had already happened. Where I would go to school, what subjects I would take, who I would marry, and how many kids we'd have. His plan had me attending meetings to learn about the tribe's business and their quest to achieve recognition by the government. Coyote has spent his entire life working to achieve this recognition. It is the legacy he's worked toward. If he can't succeed in his lifetime, I know he'll expect Toff and me to continue the battle.

"Was Dad conscious?" Toff asks.

"For a minute," I pull out the USB drive and show it to him. "He gave me this and then muttered something about a man."

"Who?"

I shrug. "No idea. He only managed to say, 'Don't let him.' I don't know who or what he's trying to do. Maybe we'll find some answers on the drive. My brothers are meeting us at the hospital. Maybe Pirate can find something. He always has his computer with him. But for now, let's keep this between us."

Toff nods as the girls return. "Ready?"

"Okay, they'll expect you at eleven," Crow announces before we can leave. "They're happy to hear you're taking over as chief."

"You are?" Olivia asks me.

"Have to. The tribe needs a leader and expects me to step up." I take Olivia's hand and kiss her fingers. "It won't be forever, just until Dad gets out of the hospital."

Olivia nods as Annette studies me. I give her a questioning look, but she shakes her head and turns her attention to Toff.

"You guys take off. I'll come to the hospital after the cops finish here," Crow says.

The engine's hum is the only sound during the forty-minute drive to the hospital. We're all lost in our thoughts. I glance at Olivia often to make sure she's not sleeping. I'm still not convinced she doesn't have a concussion, even though she isn't showing the signs. She's staring out the window, her eyes open as she chews on her bottom lip. I feel guilty for not paying her more attention. Lifting her hand, I kiss her knuckles.

"You doing okay, baby?" I ask her.

She jolts but smiles at me. "I am. I'm just coming to terms with everything that's happened today. It's a lot."

I grunt in agreement.

"Do you think our kidnapping has anything to do with the attack on your father?"

I sense Toff and Annette stiffen as they tune into our conversation. "I don't know. Seems like it should. I can't imagine we're facing more than one enemy. However, we won't know until we figure out who attacked the chief."

"Once you become chief, do you think whoever attacked him will come after you, too?"

Chapter Twenty: Olivia

This has been the week from hell. Forget that. I am in hell. That's the only explanation for all the shit that's happened this week. Almost getting kidnapped, then getting kidnapped, and now the brutal attack on Lake's father. Those are just the highlights. Now, Lake has agreed to step up as chief. I don't know what that means. Is he now in danger, too? Not that I don't think he can handle himself, but whoever attacked Coyote stabbed him in the back. Did his attacker sneak up on him? Or is it as I fear? That Coyote knew and trusted his attacker?

Lake startles me when he lifts my hand to kiss my knuckles. "You doing okay, baby?"

I offer him a smile, even though I can't find anything to smile about. "I am. I'm just coming to terms with everything that's happened today. It's a lot. Do you think our kidnapping has anything to do with the attack on your father?"

"I don't know. Seems like it should. I can't imagine we're facing more than one enemy. However, we won't know until we figure out who attacked Coyote."

"Once you become chief, do you think whoever attacked him will come after you, too?" Because that is my second biggest fear. My first? That I'll lose him once he becomes chief. It isn't that I'm not worried about his safety. It's just that Lake won't turn his back on anyone after the attack on Coyote. So, no, my primary concern isn't Lake's safety. I'm worried about how his becoming chief will impact our relationship. Maybe I'm being selfish. This is likely only temporary, but I can't help but feel I've already lost him.

"I hope he does. I want to get my hands on him. But hey, you don't have to worry about me. Whoever attacked Coyote caught him by surprise. He won't find me an easy target."

I nodded in agreement because I'd already come to that conclusion. "When those guys locked us in the cellar, they said we were serving as a distraction."

Lake nods. "That makes sense. The entire tribe was out looking for you at our request. That allowed someone an opportunity to attack Coyote without being seen."

"They also said someone wanted us," Annette chimes in.

"She's right. The leader mentioned it. He stopped one of our kidnappers from hitting Annette because he didn't want to lose the payday."

I hear Toff growl, but I'm watching Lake. His jaw clenches, and I can see his mind working. I don't know what he's thinking, but the thoughts are dark. He says nothing more until we get to the hospital.

Lake pulls me to him once we exit the vehicle. He slows down to let Toff and Annette get inside first. "I've called Hex. He and the others are on their way here. I want you to go back to the clubhouse with them."

I stiffen at his words. Is this it? He's sending me back to New Orleans so he can stay here? I wonder if he'll tell me it's over or have Hex deliver the news. Or maybe Levi?

Lake gives me a shake. "Olivia? Are you alright? Is it the concussion? Are you feeling dizzy?"

"No. I'm fine. Let's go inside."

But Lake doesn't let it go. He tugs my hand to keep me from walking away and pulls me back towards him. He captures my face in his hands as he stares into my eyes. "What just happened there? I lost you for a minute. Where did you go?"

I try to shake my head, but his grasp is too firm. "It's nothing…" I start, making him frown as his hold on me tightens.

"Olivia. I can't fix the problem if I don't know what it is. Please. Talk to me."

"I don't want to lose you," I whisper.

"Why would you lose me? Are you still worried that whoever attacked Coyote will come after me? You know I can take care of myself."

"That isn't it. You're staying here and taking on the role your father wants you to inherit. You want me to leave. What does this mean for us? Are you staying here permanently? Are we over?"

"Oh, sweet girl, we aren't over. We'll never be over. I love you. A hospital parking lot isn't where I wanted to say it, but I think you need to hear it. I'll do what I must for my tribe, but this is not where my life is. My life is in New Orleans with the Demon Dawgs and with you. I have a plan, but I need you to trust me." He glances up to look inside the hospital before looking back at me. "Toff is the man the tribe needs as chief. They aren't ready to accept him. Yet. But I also don't want him taking on the role until we know who attacked Coyote. I'll be their chief until Coyote heals or until we find out who attacked him. Then, Toff can take back what is rightfully his. Okay?"

Wrapping my arms around him, I bury my face in his chest and breathe in the woodsy scent of Lake. "I'm sorry, I'm being so selfish. The thought of losing you…"

"You have nothing to be sorry for. Everything has happened so quickly. We're all just trying to stay one step ahead. You aren't losing me. You're stuck with me until you no longer want me."

Leaning up, I kiss his chin before snuggling back into his chest. "I guess you'll be with me forever, then. I love you, too."

Lake slams his lips down on mine. We get lost in each other until Toff steps back outside and calls out. Breaking apart, Lake takes my hand and leads me inside. I move toward the waiting room where Toff and Annette have found seats, but Lake pulls me to the check-in desk. A young nurse sits next to a security guard. They both stare at Lake. The nurse eyes him like he's a giant chocolate bar she wants to take a bite of, whereas the security guard looks like he's debating on calling for reinforcements.

"My woman has a gash on her head. We don't think she has a concussion, but we need the doctor to examine her."

"Of course," the nurse simpers, shoving a clipboard into my hands without taking her eyes off Lake. Shaking my head, I pick up a pen. Since no one else is waiting, I fill in the form at the desk, letting the nurse finish eye-fucking Lake. What? Knowing someone else envies what I've got is a significant confidence boost. Handing the clipboard back, I glanced up at Lake, who smirked. He ignores the nurse but leans over to kiss me.

"We could have sat down to fill in the forms," he says, leading me toward Toff and Annette.

"We could have, but she looked bored. Thought she might appreciate the distraction."

"Dad's in surgery," Toff says when we reach him. "The nurse said someone will come out to update us."

We're the only four people in the waiting room, so I'm not surprised when the nurse calls my name minutes after we're seated. Lake stands to go with me, but the roar of motorcycles announces the arrival of the Demon Dawgs.

"That's probably Hex and the others," Lake says, glancing toward the door.

"Go talk to them. I'll be fine." He kisses me and watches me disappear behind the doors.

"I hear you have a nasty gash on your head," the doctor says when he enters the exam room. He's attractive with thick black hair, including a touch of gray at the temples. He has a copper skin tone, similar to Lake's but lighter, something you'd expect for someone who likely spends his days indoors. He's handsome. I imagine many of the nurses and patients find him irresistible. He goes through the standard questions one asks to determine if a patient suffers from a concussion. I assure him I'm not.

"I'm surprised Annette suggested you come in," he says, giving me a quick grin when I look at him in surprise. "Annette's my daughter. I'm Dr. Antoine Solon. You must be Olivia? Annette called me and told me what happened to you both."

"Annette saved our lives. I couldn't have escaped without her help. She led us through the swamp until Toff and Lake discovered us."

"Annette knows that area well. She loves the bayou. I guess that's why she wants to take over the clinic."

"You don't sound happy about her decision."

"I'm not, but she's loyal to the tribe."

"You're not?"

He shrugs. "They're my people, and I admire them, but I don't want her to take over the clinic. Especially after what happened to Dr. Sinclair."

"Lake and Toff are trying to discover who attacked him. We think they might be the same men who kidnapped Annette and me. If they can find and stop them, she'll be safe when she takes over the clinic."

"And the person who attacked Coyote? Are the same men responsible for that, too?"

The answer to that question is a resounding no. Coyote wouldn't have turned his back on those men.

Chapter Twenty-One: Lake

In the parking lot, I find Hex, Pirate, and Zip. After a greeting that consists of bumping shoulders and slapping backs, I feel a sense of calm wash over me. Having them around me made me realize how vulnerable I'd felt, exposed, like a raw nerve. I can handle myself, but having my brothers beside me makes me feel invincible. With them, I know we can figure out what the fuck is going on, and together, we can fix it.

"How's Olivia and your dad?" Hex asks.

"Dad's in surgery. They just took Olivia to check her for a concussion. The bullet grazed Olivia's scalp when those assholes shot at them. She's not showing the signs, but I wanted them to check her out."

"Well, you managed to wing one of them, so that's a start. But you can pay them back later." Hex slaps my back.

"You caught them?"

"Damn straight. We waited at the convenience store. I figured they'd drive right by, and we'd follow them. However, they stopped to fill up. One went inside to grab rubbing alcohol and bandages. We grabbed him in the bathroom while he was treating his wound. We ambushed the second guy when he came in to check on the first. Then we took out the third. It was almost too easy."

"That convenience store has cameras," I remind them.

Pirate chuckles. "I'd planned to block them, but the kid behind the counter turned them off when we entered. He recognized our kuttes from when you stopped by. I think he was hoping we came to do what we did."

"Piled them up into the SUV, along with their bikes. Levi and Jack drove them back to the clubhouse. Dixie and Abra are working on them with strict orders not to push them too far. They know you want a piece of them."

"Who the fuck are they?" I ask before remembering the pamphlet Toff found. Pulling it out, I hand it to Hex. "Found this where they held Olivia and Annette."

"Keepers of the Third Reich? What kind of fucked up racist bullshit is this?" Hex says, handing the pamphlet to Pirate.

"Don't know, but the address on that pamphlet is Nevada. Maybe Puma's heard of them?"

"I'll give him a call. See if he's heard of these fuckers. But if their base is in Nevada, what the fuck are they doing here?"

"Are these the same assholes who are harassing Francois and the others?" Zip asks, frowning.

"Olivia said she didn't recognize the men, but she did recognize the kuttes."

"Could they be the ones who attacked your dad?" Hex asks.

"Don't know." I lead them inside the hospital and over to Toff and Annette. They've all met Toff before, so I introduce Annette to them.

"You saw the blood pooling around Coyote. How long would you say since he'd been lying there?" I ask Annette.

"Based on the clotting, he hadn't been lying there for more than five minutes. I'm surprised you didn't run into his attacker. Do you think the men who kidnapped us attacked Coyote?"

"Toff and Lake saw them heading for New Orleans," Pirate chimes in.

"Besides, someone would have seen or heard the motorcycles at Dad's place," Toff says. "Our people are watching for them after what's been happening. Someone would have called us if they had. The town searched for Annette and Olivia so that someone would have seen them."

"Maybe we can ask during the meeting tomorrow," I muse.

"What meeting?" Hex asks.

I tell him about my taking on the role of chief with Coyote out of commission and about the town meeting we're holding in the morning to announce the appointment.

"You sure that's what you want to do?" Hex asks, watching me.

"What I want to do? No, but it's what I need to do. For now." I flick a glance at Toff.

Hex nods, understanding what I'm not saying. The real reason I'm stepping up is that Toff doesn't. I don't know who attacked Coyote. But if they attacked him because he's the tribal chief, I sure as hell am not going to let Toff put himself in harm's way.

"Any thoughts on why someone attacked Coyote?" Zip asks.

I shrug but then remember the USB drive. Digging it out of my pocket, I hold it up. "Coyote was holding this when I found him. He pressed it into my hand before passing out."

"Dad," Annette says, standing and going to hug the man walking with Olivia.

"Dr. Solon. How is my girl?" I ask, drawing Olivia to my side.

"After everything she's been through? Phenomenal," Dr. Solon says, shaking my hand. "Good to see you, Lake. It's been too long."

I introduce him to Hex and the others before he sits next to Annette.

"Do you have an update on Coyote?" Toff asks him.

"The last I heard, he was still in surgery. They'll let me know once he gets out. What happened?"

I go through everything again for Dr. Solon. Not only giving him the details about finding Coyote but also about what we've learned about the assholes who kidnapped Annette and Olivia and who have been threatening the tribe.

"Are you certain they didn't attack Coyote?"

"Toff and I saw the men who kidnapped the women leaving Running Bear's land. They headed for the main road leading out of town. They wouldn't have had time to come back and attack Coyote. Why?"

"I spoke to Dr. Sinclair when he was in the hospital. He told me all that he remembered about the attack. He confirmed the men who attacked him spouted off racist insults so that meshes. However, I think there is more to it than simple racism," Dr. Solon says.

"You spoke to him about the attack?" I ask.

"I treated him when they brought him in. He stayed here for a few days before they released him."

"I thought they caught him by surprise?" Annette asks.

"They did, but he regained consciousness while they ransacked the place. He pretended to be unconscious so they wouldn't do more damage. They roughed him up. He had a broken rib, a broken wrist, and a dislocated arm. They kicked the shit out of him. Bruised his kidney."

"Shit," Zip mutters while Hex takes out his phone. When he finishes texting, he gives me a nod. I smirked, knowing he just gave Abra and Dixie a laundry list of the damages they should inflict on our guests.

"So, what did he overhear?" I ask.

"They joked about getting paid for taking out a few injuns. How pleased the general was going to be when they achieved their mission along with a nice payday. And that getting rid of the injuns would make everything easier for them. No witnesses."

I catch Hex's eye. Even though we don't speak, the communication is there. Our list of questions for the racist pricks grows longer. I'm debating returning to New Orleans and postponing the meeting with the elders until I know more about our enemies. However, I know part of why I want to delay the meeting is because I'm not looking forward to taking on the mantle worn by my father. I swore I'd never accept the responsibility of being the chief of our tribe. The role laid out by my father and my ancestors. A role that would fit as uneasily as life inside a cubicle wearing a suit and tie. I study Toff, whose attention shifts from Annette to her father and the door leading into the hospital. The leadership of our tribe belongs on his shoulders, but not yet. I hope my decision to take over temporarily doesn't obliterate any chance of Coyote seeing Toff's worth.

"Why did you ask if the men who kidnapped us were the ones who attacked Coyote?" Annette asks her father.

"Because the men who hurt Dr. Sinclair commented about scalping the chief. I know someone stabbed Coyote, but I wondered if they'd gone after him."

I clench my fists. Scalping. Not something our tribe practiced, but something I will gladly use to torture those motherfuckers.

Pirate, oblivious to the conversation as he read through what was on the USB drive, leans back in his chair.

"Find something?" I ask him.

"Maybe. There is a bunch of information about the tribe on this drive. I'm just not sure what it all means."

"Let me take a look," Toff offers, sitting next to Pirate and sliding the laptop over. He reads for a few minutes before glancing at me, then Antoine.

"Coyote has put together his case to take to the BIA. Bureau of Indian Affairs," he clarifies. "To achieve recognition, the tribe has to meet seven criteria. He has them all mapped out on this drive. He has the name of a lawyer based in New Orleans, and he is working with her on this. Rey Montague. We need to talk to her. In five days, Coyote has a calendar entry for a meeting with the Office of Federal Acknowledgement to present the completed petition."

"I didn't realize he was so close," Solon mutters. "Your father's been working on this for most of his life. He wants the recognition to be the legacy he leaves behind. Having it would protect the tribe and our land."

"Which is critical, considering the other document I found on the drive," Pirate continues. "A request to perform a geological survey on the land."

Chapter Twenty-Two: Olivia

"What does that mean?" Annette asks. "What are they looking for?"

"Oil, most likely," Zip says. "Louisiana is a major producer of oil in this country. They have rigs on and off-shore. BOEM has a map of all the rigs. Pull it up."

Pirate hits a few keys before turning the laptop so we can all see. Icons representing what I assume are oil rigs fill the screen. There are a few empty areas, the largest being the area surrounding Lake's tribe.

"Coyote's trying to keep them from drilling on our land," Toff says.

"Or making sure the tribe keeps the rights to the oil," Hex adds.

Toff reels back in anger. "Dad wouldn't do that."

"Why not?" Lake asks. "It would mean more money for the tribe."

"But it would destroy our way of life. Coyote would never allow that to happen, no matter how much money it brought in. It would be a betrayal to the tribe and our ancestors."

Lake nods before clasping Toff on the back. "You're right. But that doesn't mean others won't think differently."

"You think this is why someone attacked Coyote?" I ask. "Because he's trying to protect the land?"

Lake nods. "It makes the most sense. The skinheads said someone was paying them to drive the tribe off the land. Whoever it is either has the money to pay them or expects to come into money. Driving the tribe off the land would allow an oil company to come in and take what they want. These assholes have been threatening the tribe, but no one shows signs of leaving. Whoever is paying them might be getting desperate."

"You think a stranger came into town and attacked Coyote?" Toff asks, shaking his head. "No fucking way. Someone would have seen a stranger or an unknown vehicle. Remember, the tribe was out looking for Annette and Olivia. Someone would have seen something and called us."

"You think a member of the tribe attacked Coyote?" Dr. Solon asks.

Toff nods slowly. "Whoever attacked Coyote stabbed him in the back. Coyote wouldn't turn his back on a stranger. But a friend? A member of the tribe?"

I look at Lake and see the resignation. He'd already considered the possibility. Why hadn't he said anything? In addition to resignation, I see sadness. Following his gaze, I look at Toff. He's the reason. Lake was trying to protect Toff from realizing a member of the tribe attacked their father. Taking Lake's hand, I squeeze it. I'm trying to offer him some comfort.

Lake is mentally and physically strong. His confidence and competence run deep. His shoulders are broad, and I know he thinks he can carry the world's weight on them. But not even Atlas himself could support the pressure Lake is under. He glances at me and smiles, but the smile remains sad. Feeling guilty about my meltdown in the parking lot, I sit on his lap, wrapping my arms around those broad shoulders and nuzzling his neck.

"We're going to get through this," I whisper. "You aren't alone. Toff needs to face the facts. You can't protect him from the truth. Let us help you. All of us. We're all on your side."

Lake kisses the top of my head.

Hearing a noise, I glance over Lake's shoulder to see a doctor approaching us. I pat Lake's chest before climbing off his lap.

"Dr. Martinez," Dr. Solon calls out in greeting.

"Peridot family?" Dr. Martinez asks—his attention on Lake, who nods.

"I'm his son, Lake, my brother, Two-Feathers. How is he?"

"He's stable. We were able to repair the damage done by the knife and replace the blood he lost. He's recovering, and we'll move him into a room in a few hours. You can see him if you'd like. He hasn't gained consciousness and probably won't tonight."

Lake and Toff follow Dr. Martinez.

"I should probably get back to work," Dr. Solon says, squeezing

Annette's arm. "You're headed to New Orleans tomorrow, right?"

Annette jolts. "I forgot. Yes. I start work at Tulane the day after tomorrow. I need to move into my apartment tomorrow."

"Tulane Hospital?" Hex asks, glancing at me.

"Annette is doing her residency there. We'll be working together," I tell him.

"You know about what almost happened to Olivia, right?" Hex asks.

His question has Dr. Solon stopping and turning back to our little group. "What happened?"

Hex explains about my missing friends and how someone tampered with my car before trying to kidnap me. "The cops are finally making some headway. An anonymous caller had them questioning Olivia's patient. The cops got her statement along with the statement of the man who intervened. They also have a report from the car repair shop about the sabotage. They're linking several disappearances together and think they're after a gang of men who are targeting young women, mostly pregnant women."

"Maybe you should postpone your residency," Solon says. "Or find a different hospital."

"I can't, Dad. You know I can't do that. Look, I'll be careful. Olivia already warned me. My apartment is only a few blocks from the hospital."

"I don't like it. Maybe Toff can…"

"No, don't say anything to Toff. He has enough to deal with right now."

"We can carpool," I offer. "I don't know if we can get on the same shifts, but we can try."

"What if they figure out where you live?"

"You can stay at the clubhouse," Hex cuts in. "Olivia is staying there. We have a room available. A prospect will be driving Olvia to and from work. They can drive you, too. You don't have to worry about being on the same shift. We have enough people to drive both of you."

"I admit I'd feel better," Solon says, looking at Annette. "Please."

Annette glances at me. "How bad is it?"

"Not quite as bad as a frat house, but close," I admit, causing Hex to smirk. "However, the food is fantastic. Nora, who does all the cooking, is about to open a restaurant. Hex's mom and girlfriend live there, so it's fairly tame."

"Well, I don't think I'll be spending much time there, in any case.

Residents don't sleep, right, Dad?"

"True. But I'd feel better knowing you had these guys looking out for you." He hugs his daughter and leaves us.

"Thanks," Annette says to Hex. "You don't have to open your home to me, but I appreciate it."

"No problem. You're friends with Lake and we take care of our own. Do you need any help moving?"

"No, I wasn't going to take anything more than clothes. I'll pack tonight and drive to New Orleans in the morning."

"I'll go with you," I tell her. "Lake wants me to return to the clubhouse."

"Lake will probably come to the clubhouse tomorrow or the next day," Hex says.

"Why?" I ask.

"Let's just say he has some business to attend to. Club business," he adds when I open my mouth to ask.

I close my mouth, knowing that there is no sense in asking. When the guys say club business, the walls go up, and they're impenetrable.

When Lake and Toff return to the waiting room, Annette and I rush over to them. They both look exhausted.

"How is he?" Annette asks.

"He's still unconscious. He looks so frail in that hospital bed with all the wires coming out of him," Lake says with a shudder. "I've never seen him look weak."

"He'll get better," Annette assures him. "Just give him some time to recover."

"I'm staying here. His attacker may show up to finish the job," Lake says.

"I already called Conor and Danny to come here and stand guard. You have other responsibilities to take care of with your father laid up. I'm returning to New Orleans, but Zip is staying with you."

"Thanks, Prez," Lake says, shaking Hex's hand.

"Annette and Olivia are coming to the clubhouse tomorrow. Annette's staying with us while she's doing her residency. Figured that should keep you both from worrying."

Lake smacks Hex on the back while Toff shakes Hex's hand. "Thanks, man."

"How about I drive," Annette offers. "You two look ready to drop. Zip, you can stay in my guest room."

Zip follows us back to Annette's house. While Annette shows him to his room, I take Lake to the one we share.

"I'm exhausted, but I need you," Lake says, pulling me in for a hug. His hands wander over my back before shifting down to my butt. He squeezes my cheeks as he grinds his lengthening cock into my belly. My core tightens with the feel of him. He isn't the only one with needs.

Leaning back, I slide my hands under his shirt and lift. "How about I do all the work," I suggest as he pulls the shirt off. His eyes brighten with my suggestion.

"Oh, yeah? You gonna ride me, my beautiful girl?"

Chapter Twenty-Three: Lake

While I tug off my shirt, Olivia's nimble fingers unfasten my belt. The hunger in her eyes has my dick pressing painfully against the zipper. Relief comes when she pushes my jeans and boxers to the floor. I let her push me to the edge of the bed before I fall back. Taking my cock in hand, I stroke it as I watch her strip for me. First, she loses the top but leaves on the pale pink satin bra that glows against her olive skin. I groan as she exposes her gorgeous body. My eyes feast on her as she loses the matching panties and, finally, that sexy bra.

"Come here and sit on my face," I order. Grinning at her full-body shiver.

Placing one knee on the bed between my legs, she crawls up my body, pausing long enough to lick the pre-cum off my hardened dick. I shudder at the feel of her mouth on me, but I want to be the one to make her shudder.

Grabbing her by the waist, I place her right where I want her. Burying my face in her sweet-smelling pussy rejuvenates me. All the stress of today evaporates as I lose myself in the taste of my woman. Her moans and whimpers as I lick and nibble on her clit are like a live wire in my system. Soon, she's grinding on my face, searching for her release. Too soon, her body quakes with the impact of her orgasm.

Snagging a condom, I tear it open. Olivia snatches it out of my hands and then sits on my legs. Placing the condom on the tip, she uses her mouth to sheathe me. "Fuck, baby," I groan as I struggle to keep from embarrassing myself.

She lifts her head and grins at me, the little imp. Planting her pussy alongside my cock, she wraps her hands around it so she can glide up and down. Holy shit, the woman is trying to kill me. "Baby, I need you to ride me. Need to see those breasts jiggle."

Putting me out of my misery, she lines her slit over my cock and impales herself. Her long groan of pleasure has my hips jerking in response. Planting her hands on my chest, she fucks herself on my cock. Grabbing her hips, I increase the pace until her titties sway and jump in my face. Mesmerized, I can't tear my eyes off the beauty before me. Squeezing her ass makes her groan loader as her juices flood over my cock. Sliding my finger down the crack of her ass, I press against her tight bud.

"I'm going to take you there one day," I warn her before pressing my finger inside. She shudders and cries out as the pleasure washes over her as the orgasm rips through her system. Taking over, I piston into her, my eyes on her beautiful face until I explode inside her.

"Oh, shit," Olivia mutters as she collapses on top of me. "If you taking my ass is half as erotic as you talking about it, sign me up."

She mumbles her words into my chest, but I hear them. Chuckling, I roll her to the side so I can get up and dispose of the condom. When I return, she's in the same spot I left her. Chuckling, I gather her up in my arms and cradle her with one hand while pulling down the sheets. Tucking us both under the covers, she murmurs as she snuggles into me.

Even though I'm exhausted, I lay awake. My mind goes over everything that happened today, and I think about what tomorrow will bring. Becoming chief is a role I've avoided, but I'm willingly stepping into it tomorrow. Even telling myself that it's only temporary doesn't relieve the tightness in my chest.

I must eventually doze off, but a dream about drowning in paperwork has me gasping for breath.

It doesn't take a therapist to explain the meaning. Years of watching my father dealing with paperwork and attending endless tribal meetings gave me a clear idea of what my life would hold if I followed his path. His repeated insistence that I learn my role early to become a better leader in the future gave me the impetus to forge my path in a different direction.

Carefully, I slide out from under Olivia. Leaving her to sleep, I quickly shower and change before heading downstairs. I find Zip already up and drinking a cup of coffee. He has several colored pencils and a few sheets of paper in front of him. Something that is not uncommon. As a tattooist, he's often sketching out ideas. However, when I sit down, I see he's drawing a map. This, too, isn't unusual. Zip's hobby is cartography. His work is detailed and stunning. One of his best pieces, a map of New Orleans, holds pride of place in his office.

I watched him work and realized that his map depicted tribal land. He's completed the mainland and has moved on to the bayou. As he draws, he refers to his laptop.

"What are you doing?" I ask him.

"Mapping out the bayou." I roll my eyes before he continues. "I had a thought when I was looking at the BOEM map. Who patrols the area?"

"You mean the bayou? I guess the Coast Guard. Why?"

"No, I mean the tribal lands. Does the tribe have a police presence?"

I shake my head. "No. The Sheriff has jurisdiction. Why?"

"Would you say they have a strong presence?"

I chuckle. "No. We get a few patrol cars occasionally coming through, but for the most part, they let us police ourselves."

"That's what I thought. If the chief gains recognition from the US government, they'll get funding for a tribal police force. It might not be more than a handful of cops, but they'll provide more coverage than the Sheriff currently covers. Right?"

I slowly nod as I consider the additional ramifications of tribal recognition. "You think someone doesn't want that to happen?"

"I think it's a possibility." He flips the paper around and hands me a red pencil. "Can you draw the boundaries of the land your people own?"

I take the pencil and outline the area from memory. Drawing the property lines on the mainland is easy, but I have difficulty remembering how many islands belong to the tribe. I slide it back to Zip when I think I've done a decent job. "I think that's right. It's been a while since I lived here, but property doesn't change hands often. What are you thinking?"

"Your people own a direct path between the mainland and the Gulf of Mexico. It's a smuggler's dream. Look at all the locations where they could hide merchandise." Using his finger, he indicates a path through the bayou that passes by various tribal landholds. Once they reach the mainland, they have direct access to the highways and backroads to move it."

I studied the areas he pointed out and realized that Pieter's land is the perfect location for moving cargo into or out of tribal territory. Joseph's land is on the water and connected to Pieter's land via a tiny sliver of swampland. Is that why the skinheads focused their attention on these two families?

"Remember, I told you about the Oxbridge's and the Billiot's?"

"The families harassed by the men we have at The Farm?"

"Yes. These are their landholds." I point to the two locations.

Zip nods. "If I was setting up a smuggling operation, these are the two places I'd need. Look at them. They're perfect. I'm guessing they have at least a house on each plot?" I nod. "Perfect for storing goods. Cut a path through the swamp, and they'd have easy access between the two properties. The area's remote. How much do you want to bet the Sheriff doesn't spend much time patrolling this far out?"

"Wouldn't make that bet. Shit. Do you think that's what the skinheads are doing? They want the land to use for smuggling?"

"I'd say it's a good possibility. Especially if we consider what Dr. Sinclair overheard, say their leader sent them here to establish a smuggling route but somehow got involved with whoever wanted to exploit the land for oil. How perfect would that be? The oil company would come in and set up rigs, leaving the skinheads free reign for their smuggling efforts."

"Both plans would fall apart if Coyote managed to convince the government to recognize our tribe. But there is no way these guys attacked Coyote. You guys shipped them off to The Farm before the attack."

"What's The Farm, and who did you ship there?" Toff asks, coming into the kitchen and going toward the coffee maker.

Zip and I both grimace before turning to face Toff. Neither of us says anything, which has Toff turning to study us. "Well?"

"It's club business," I tell him.

Toff studies me before returning to the coffeemaker and pouring himself a mug. He turns back. "I'm your brother. You can trust me."

"Yes, you are, and yes, I can, but it's safer for you and us if you don't know. Just drop it. Okay?"

Chapter Twenty-Four: Olivia

I wake up cold, so I know Lake's no longer in bed. Rolling over, I feel the sheets and realize he's been gone for some time. Checking my phone, I expect the time to be much later than seven. Rolling out of bed, I shower and pack my clothes and toiletries. Annette and I are driving back to New Orleans today, and I want to be ready to leave. Stepping out my door, I run into Toff, who is leaving Annette's room. He gives me a guilty look before hightailing it downstairs. Annette smirks at me.

"I thought you two were a couple," I tease her as we follow him.

"He didn't want to be alone last night."

I can only nod at that statement. The previous day was tough for Toff. From the sound of raised voices from the kitchen, today is off to a bad start for him, too.

"Just drop it. Okay?" Lake snaps.

"What's going on?" I ask Lake, eyeing the two brothers as they glare at each other.

"Lake's spouting his club business bullshit," Toff says, not taking his eyes off his brother. "He said they shipped someone off to a farm but won't say who or what this fucking farm is."

I whip my head around to stare at Lake. "You caught them?"

Lake growls, but Zip chuckles. "You might as well tell them. They'll work it out eventually. Besides, I'm sure they'd all like to know they don't have to keep looking over their shoulders."

Lake glances at Zip, then shrugs. "Fine. You're right. Okay, yesterday, after we saw the three men who kidnapped Olivia and Annette take off from Running Bear's cabin, I called Hex. They intercepted the men, took them somewhere, and locked them up. I'm not telling you anything more."

"I take it this 'farm' is where your enemies disappear?" Annette asks.

"What part of my statement that I'm not telling you anything more did you not understand?" Lake demands.

Annette glances at me, then Toff, before returning to Lake. "Can you promise those assholes aren't going to bother us or our people again? You don't have to speak. A nod will do."

Lake gives her a quick nod.

"Then, I'm fine with you keeping your secrets. Three assholes off the streets and out of our lives is payment enough."

Lake shifts his eyes to Toff. The stubborn set of his jaw tells me he isn't as agreeable as Annette, but he surprises me by shrugging. "I don't like it. Those assholes should pay for what they did, but I doubt the cops will do more than smack them on the wrist. I have one more question, and then I'm done."

Lake sighed but gestured for him to continue.

"Are you going to find out why they threatened our people and kidnapped the women?"

"We are, but I think Zip already figured out what they wanted with our land. Zip?"

Zip pushes the paper in front of him to the other side of the table so we can see it.

"This is amazing. Did you draw it?" Annette asks, eyeing the colored pencils.

"Zip's hobby is cartography," I explain. "You should see the map he created of New Orleans. It hangs up in his office. The detail is stunning."

"The line here is our territory, right?" Toff asks, pointing to the red lines that dissect the map. The poorly drawn lines stand out against the carefully drawn map.

"As close as I could make them," Lake says.

"Are they correct?" Zip asks.

"Close enough. The only change is here," Toff says, pointing to the line that passes through the bayou. "These two islands are owned by two of our families."

"Okay, let me adjust," Zip says, pulling the map back and redrawing the lines. He turns the map back around and explains how ideal the setup is for smuggling.

"That makes sense," Toff admits. "Most of our people make their living in the bayou. They harvest their products from the sea and transport them to buyers via the mainland. No one pays them any mind because they've been traveling the same route for decades. The Sheriff leaves us alone because we've never given him cause to think we're doing anything illegal."

"That would change if Coyote achieves recognition for our tribe. As an official tribe, we could install a police force. We'd have tribal police patrolling the area. They'd notice if strangers were using our land and roads," Annette adds.

"That was our thinking, too."

"So, the person who attacked Coyote was trying to stop his progress for either the smuggling or the oil. What are we going to do to figure out who and why?" Toff asks.

"I'll present everything we know and suspect to the elders today and then to the rest of our people," Lake says. "I don't know why Coyote kept it secret, but he put himself at risk by not sharing his plan."

"You think by bringing it out into the open, Coyote's attacker will expose himself?" I ask.

"I think by bringing it out into the open and announcing that I'm taking over the legal battle, whoever attacked Coyote will come after me."

I jerk at his comment. He wraps his arm around my shoulders and draws me close. "Don't worry about me. I can take care of myself. Plus, knowing I'm a target makes me more dangerous to them than they are to me."

I know he is right; someone with eyes in the back of their head would have the advantage in a fight. Whoever came after Lake wouldn't find him as easy a target as Coyote. Knowing this eased some of the worry, but not all of it. "You're staying to watch his back?" I ask Zip.

Zip grins. "You know it. We look out for each other. Your man will be safe."

"We should get going," Annette says. "I'm hoping we can go to the hospital so I can sign in."

"Levi is on his way to pick you up," Lake says. He holds his hand up when Annette opens her mouth to protest. "I know you want to take your car, but you'll be safer driving with him. You won't need your car in the short term. The prospects will drive you everywhere."

"I still want my car," Annette pushes back.

"How about I drop it off?" Toff offers. "I'm calling the lawyer who was working with Coyote. If I meet her at her office, I can take your car. I'd like to see the clubhouse and the hospital where you will work."

Annette grins. "I'd like that. Okay, I can survive a day or two without a vehicle. You sure we can trust Levi?"

"Since he's my brother, yes," I say with a laugh.

The men leave for the meeting with the elders before Levi arrives to pick us up. After I introduced Levi and Annette, he helped load up the SUV with her bags.

"Cleo and Delphine have readied a room for you," Levi says once we're on the road. "Nora is cooking a special dinner for tonight to welcome you. Everyone is excited to have you stay."

Annette looks shocked and pleased. "That's very nice of you. I admit I was a little concerned about staying in an apartment alone. While at school, I had roommates. First in the dorm and then in an apartment. Then, after hearing about the kidnappings, I was dreading being on my own."

"You don't have to worry about that now," I assure her. "There is always someone around the clubhouse."

The drive back to New Orleans is uneventful. I haven't lived at the clubhouse long, so I remember my awe at seeing the former plantation. Hex has a photo of the house when it was new: impeccably maintained grounds with pristine gardens. I can't help but remember that when they took that photo, misery had created the opulence. I much prefer the natural wildness that surrounds the place now. Hex has a few framed photos of the enslaved people who toiled on this land. Pictures meant to capture the prosperity of the plantation owner but now were symbols of respect for those who had no voice. Nature reclaiming the land shows the power of freedom.

"This is an MC clubhouse?" Annette asks. "How did they acquire an old plantation?"

I chuckle at her disbelief. "Hex's family once lived here."

"So, he inherited the land?"

"No. Hex's ancestors were enslaved people on the land. He bought it and turned it into a symbol of freedom. Because that's what the MC life is all about. Freedom. Freedom to live your life the way you want to live it."

Levi unloads Annette's bags while I lead her to the front door. We step inside to find Delphine and Cleo waiting for us.

"Annette, this is Cleo. She's Hex's woman. And this is Delphine. She's Hex's mother. Her man is Dixie, who you haven't met yet.

"Did someone say my name?" comes an Irish lilt behind us. Turning, I spot Dixie coming down the stairs along with Abra. After introducing Annette to them, we sit on the couches in the corner of the grand room. The news is on, and the flashing headline and the photo of a woman I recognize capture my attention. My friend Talia. The nurse who has been missing for several weeks. The headline proclaims that the police found the body of the missing woman floating in the river.

Chapter Twenty-Five: Lake

The elders met in a small conference room beside the high school gymnasium. I'd attended a few of these meetings when Coyote was grooming me to take over. Most of those meetings were short and unmemorable. But I clearly remember one ending with me driving into New Orleans and enlisting in the Louisiana Army National Guard. That meeting had been about me and my future. They had everything mapped out and laid their expectations before me. They told me which college I'd attend and the classes I needed to take. The elders outlined my class schedule and defined how I'd spend my free time. They even presented me with a list of women, informing me to select a wife from the list. Now, here I was, a decade later, sitting in the last place I wanted to be, discussing a life I never planned on living.

"With Coyote in the hospital, I'm offering to fill in as chief until he's well again," I tell the four men and three women who comprise the council of elders. Each is the respective head of their families. These families have been leaders in our tribe for centuries.

"Why?" Asks Baptiste, the oldest of the group. His once-black hair is now all gray. His face is a map of wrinkles from working on shrimping boats his entire life. He had been on the council when Coyote brought me to the meetings. "You never seemed interested in leading our tribe before. So why now? Why not Toff? He'd make a better chief."

I almost smirk at that. For years, I've tried and failed to convince my father that Toff is the better choice. Now that I'm willing to step up and assume the role, the people who can stop me recognize what I've known all along. But I need them to agree to this plan to protect their future chief.

"You're right; Toff is a better choice, but not right now. Not after what happened to Coyote. I'll explain." I take the time to lock eyes with each council member. I need them to see that I'm not bullshitting them and that what I have to say is not only accurate but unpleasant. "Whoever attacked Coyote wasn't an outsider. He was someone Coyote knew. This person entered Coyote's home under the guise of friendship before stabbing him in the back and leaving him to die."

Baptiste narrows his eyes at me. "You're lying. No one would want to hurt the chief."

"Someone does, and I have a pretty good idea about why they did it." Then, I tell them everything we know and what we suspect about the attack. As I speak, I watch each council member for their reaction. Their reaction about how close Coyote is to gaining recognition for the tribe from the government and the possibility of oil on our land. I end with the smuggling theory Zip came up with that morning.

"Although, we think those interested in using our land to smuggle goods in and out of the country may be the same men who ransacked the clinic and kidnapped Olivia and Annette."

"Maybe these men are the ones who attacked Coyote," Martine suggests. Anyone looking at her would think she was a kindly grandmother who knitted and canned vegetables. Maybe she does. I don't know. But I know she owns a fleet of fishing boats and offers tourists fishing excursions. She's one of our more wealthier members.

"They aren't. At the time of Coyote's attack, the men who kidnapped Annette and Olivia were on their way back to New Orleans."

"Besides, Coyote wouldn't have turned his back on them," Baptiste adds with a sage nod. "No, Lake is right. Coyote trusted his attacker. The only people he trusts are us, the members of his tribe."

"But why would anyone want to hurt Coyote?" Katherine, the youngest member of the council, asks.

"Isn't it obvious?" Baptiste asks, his eyes on me. "It's what Lake said about the possibility of oil in our bayou and under our homes. Once our land becomes tribal territory, no one can get that oil without going through us. Someone wants the rights to the oil and is willing to kill to get them."

"What do you suggest we do?" Martine asks me.

"Announce that we're close to achieving tribal status. We want everyone to know the progress Coyote has made. Then, explain how I'll take over as interim chief. Lastly, we'll tell them I have contacts to help us get our status sooner."

"You mean lie to them?" Baptiste asks.

"No, not lie. I do have contacts that might be able to help us," I tell them, thinking about Dante's mother, Angela Westbrook, and Cleo— women with money, power, and influence. We can solicit Puma's help, too. He'd met influential people when he was playing ball. "The important step in our plan is to ensure that whoever attacked Coyote sees me as the next target."

"You're setting yourself up as bait? Rather than Toff?" Katherine asks, catching on.

"Yes."

"What do we tell the tribe?"

"Everything. Let the tribe know what's at stake. I know Coyote wanted to keep his progress a secret, but he told someone he shouldn't have—someone who wants to stop him from succeeding. Since we don't know who that person is, we must tell everyone. We need the person who attacked Coyote to come after me, not Toff."

"Is Toff okay with you setting yourself up as bait?" Baptiste asks, watching me.

"I haven't told him that part, no, and he hasn't worked it out yet," I admit. "But Toff has an important part to play. He needs to focus on a critical piece. He'll be working with the lawyer representing our tribe. I have contacts who will help, but Toff will do most of the work."

"You consider this temporary because you expect Coyote to regain his health? What if he doesn't? Are you willing to step down and give the position to Toff?" Baptiste asks.

"Gladly. Toff's always been the better choice."

"He has," Martine says with a nod.

"Let's go, then," Baptiste says, standing and leading us to the packed gymnasium. While Baptiste explains the situation, I study their reactions. Baptiste doesn't come out and say we suspect one of them attacked Coyote, but I watch their faces when he tells them Coyote was stabbed in the back. I see and hear the realization spread through the auditorium. Gasps of surprise and angry mutterings tell me the message got through. They know we have an enemy within.

"You're saying someone attacked Coyote? One of us?" Pieter asks from his position in the center of the auditorium.

"That's what I believe," I answer. "I think someone wants to stop

Coyote from turning our land into tribal land. That someone knows oil companies are interested in drilling on our land and bayou."

"How do we protect ourselves?" Joseph asks.

"I'm taking over for Coyote. I have access to influential people who can help push this through. My goal is to achieve Coyote's dream. Nothing will stop me." I send that out as a dare. "However, we aren't only protecting our land from oil companies. I've been looking into the men who trashed our clinic and who have harassed our people. We believe these men have a different goal. You all know I belong to an MC. Our Road Captain, Zip, has come up with a possible reason these men are interested in driving some of you out of your homes. Smuggling. My club is looking into this other MC. Until Coyote leaves the hospital, I'll be your chief."

While the crowd cheers, I watch. I don't see anyone acting out of character or angry at my proclamation. However, I know not everyone is here. Toff, who stood behind me while I spoke, comes forward and clasps me on the back.

"Good speech. You'd make a good leader," he says.

"No, thanks. Once this is over, you can have it. This is your job, not mine."

"And the only reason you're doing it now is to protect me. Don't think I'm not aware of what you're doing. You think whoever attacked Coyote will come after you instead of me. That's why you're shipping me to New Orleans to meet with the lawyer."

I corrected him, "I'm shipping you off to New Orleans because you're the only one who can understand the lawyer. "

"Who are these connections you have? I hope you weren't just blowing smoke. We need all the help I can get."

"Let me contact them first to see if they will support us. If they do, I'll send them your way."

I see Crow pushing through the departing crowd. He doesn't stop until he reaches us. He's livid.

"What's wrong?" I ask.

"I stopped by to see Coyote, and your friends wouldn't let me in. What's going on?"

"That's my fault. I told them to keep everyone out but Toff and myself."

"Why?"

"For his protection."

"You think I'm a danger to Coyote? My brother?"

"No, but we don't know who attacked him right now. Coyote knew his attacker. He turned his back on him. That means someone from the tribe. I told my brothers to keep everyone out."

"That's bullshit! He's my brother!"

"Toff and I are headed to New Orleans. We'll let you know when we leave, and you can meet us at the hospital. I can take you in to see Coyote."

"Don't do me any favors," Crow snaps before leaving.

Chapter Twenty-Six: Olivia

My heart breaks as I watch the news report. My friend is no longer missing. Now she's gone. I cry as I remember the shifts we worked together and the patients we spent time with. I remember the crying sessions when the sweet little old ladies and the adorable older gentlemen we cared for passed during the night. After one too many deaths, she made a decision that would eventually result in her death. She switched hospitals and moved into obstetrics. She lasted one week before she disappeared. Now she's dead.

"I'm so sorry, Olivia," Cleo says, hugging me as I cry.

"I still hoped we'd find her."

"We all did."

"Was she one of the women who went missing?" Annette asks.

"Yes," Delphine says.

"Give me a few minutes. We can eat and then head to the hospital," I tell her.

"We don't have to go today. I can go tomorrow," Annette protests.

She thinks I'm putting her before myself, but she's wrong. I'm being very selfish. I know someone at that hospital is working with the men who kidnapped and killed my friend. They don't know it yet, but I will figure out who and make them pay.

"I want to go. I want to look each coworker in the eye and see which one isn't crying."

"Is that safe?" Cleo asks.

"You won't be going alone," Dixie says. "Levi and Jack, you take them. One stays in the SUV while the other goes with you. Don't you fucking dare let yourself be alone with any of the fuckers. Got it?"

I nod, grateful that Dixie understands how much I need to do this.

"Lunch is ready," Nora calls out as she comes out of the kitchen carrying a plate of grilled cheese sandwiches. "Can you get the soup?" she asks Levi, who dashes into the kitchen. He brings it out and places it on the table. We all take our seats and dig in. Well, almost all of us.

I only manage a few bites as I pick at my sandwich. My thoughts are on Talia. Pirate places his hand on mine to get my attention.

"After lunch, I'll access the police records and see what I can find out."

"Thank you," I tell him.

Looking around the table, I can see the men and women shooting me looks of concern. Not wanting them to worry, I force myself to join the conversation.

"Yesterday, we looked at several places for Nora's restaurant," Cleo tells Annette. "We found one with a strong possibility, but we'll look some more after lunch. Did you want to come with us?"

"That sounds like fun," Annette says, causing me to frown.

"I thought you wanted to check in at the hospital and have me show you around."

"Well, yes, but after your friend…"

"No, we'll still go. I'm okay. I am sad and furious, but I can do nothing for Talia now. I want to go to the hospital."

"Okay, then," Annette agrees.

"I can tell you what I found when you return," Pirate says.

I nod at his suggestion before forcing myself to finish my cold sandwich and even colder soup.

"Ready?" Levi asks after he helps Jack clear off the table once everyone has finished eating.

"Let me grab my jacket," Annette says, jogging up the stairs.

"You're going to be warm enough?" Levi asks me.

I'm wearing jeans and a thick sweater. "I'll be fine," I assure him.

He wraps his arms around me and holds me close. "I'm sorry about your friend, but I'm happy they didn't get their hands on you."

"Me, too," I agree. "I keep thinking about the men driving that van."

"What about them?"

"I keep thinking I should recognize them. I feel like if I had, then maybe Talia would still be alive. But I've viewed the footage multiple times. Nothing stands out."

"Maybe you should show the footage to Annette," Levi suggests.

I lean back and look at him. "Why? She doesn't know anyone at either hospital."

"She doesn't, but maybe if she sees the footage before she goes to the hospital, something might catch her eye."

"Oh, that's not a bad idea."

When Annette comes back downstairs, I run the idea past her.

"Couldn't hurt to take a look," Annette agrees, following me when Levi and I lead her down to Pirate's office. Knocking, we step in and explain what we want to try.

Pirate pulls up the video on the larger screen and lets it play. We both watched it several times. I can't shake the feeling that I know them but still can't place them. It's very frustrating.

"What is he doing?" Annette asks when we're watching the actions of the two men outside my car when they first realized I was no longer inside.

I lean in and study the image, recalling what I witnessed that night.

"He's punching his fist into his palm," I tell her. "I forgot he did that several times. I guess he was angry."

"Okay, I've seen enough. I think I'd recognize them if I saw them again. Maybe," Annette says.

"Let's head to the hospital. We'll take a tour of the building. Maybe we'll get lucky," I say as I follow Levi outside.

Once at the hospital, I accompany Annette to Human Resources, where she checks in and collects her badge. While she meets with the head of obstetrics, I sit in the hallway and watch everyone who passes by. The men who tried to kidnap me were wearing surgical scrubs, but that didn't mean they were doctors. I study the nurses, security, and the maintenance crew. I'm so focused on my search that I don't realize Annette has joined me.

"Sorry," I tell her when I realize she's been trying to gain my attention.

"That's okay. Did you recognize anyone?"

"No," I say. "Let me give you that tour."

Before taking her to the ward where she'll work, I show her the cafeteria and the doctor's lounge. To lighten our moods, I take her past the nursery so she can see the babies. We watch them briefly before moving to the nurse's station. We pass a small group of men and women led by Joyce. She shows them the nursery and explains how their babies will sleep there so they, as new mothers, can get some rest.

"What if I want the baby to be in the room with me?" asks a young black woman wearing a lavender scarf over her naturally curly hair. The scarf matches the lavender silk blouse tucked into light grey trousers and covered by a matching grey blazer.

"Of course, you can keep the baby with you," Joyce assures her. "It's encouraged, but we also want to ensure the mother is well-rested when ready to leave the hospital with her newborn."

When Joyce turns back, she sees me. Her eyes widen slightly before she nods at me and glances at Annette.

We continue to the nurse's station to find Sylvia talking with Dr. Merkel.

"Olivia!" Sylvia calls out when she sees me. "You aren't scheduled to work today."

"No, I'm not. I brought Dr. Annette Solon in for a quick tour. She's starting her residency tomorrow. Dr. Solon, this is Dr. Merkel and Sylvia Bonner."

"I heard you were starting tomorrow; it's nice to meet you. I've heard good things about you," Dr. Merkel says, shaking Annette's hand. "I look forward to working with you."

"Joyce is giving a tour for expectant mothers, but she should be wrapping that up soon. If you want to wait and meet her, too."

"We can stay a few more minutes," I assure Annette.

"Did you hear about Talia?" I ask them.

"What do you mean?"

"The police found her body."

"Oh my god, she's dead? Talia? How?"

"They haven't released the details yet."

"That's awful," Sylvia says.

"You're being careful, right?"

Sylvia gives me an odd look. "Careful? What do you mean?"

"Didn't Joyce tell you about what happened to me on the way home from my shift the other night?"

"No, what happened?"

I tell her about my near miss. Sylvia clasps her hand over her mouth, her eyes wide with fear.

"You think they work here?"

"I don't know. The two men dressed like surgeons, but they could have just stolen the gear. Keep your car keys and your phone on you. If your car breaks down, abandon it and get somewhere public."

"You know, the night Dr. Carver disappeared, I saw her car on the side of the road," Dr. Merkel says. "I wonder if that's how they got her? Maybe I should tell the police what I saw."

"That's a good idea," I tell him. Once he walks away, I turn back to Sylvia, who looks pale.

Sylvia nods. "I can't believe Joyce didn't tell me what happened. There she is. I'm going to ask her."

I turn around and freeze. Joyce is talking to a man at the end of the hallway. He has his back to us. Standing next to me, Annette gasps.

"Recognize that kutte?" I whisper. She nods slowly.

"We need to move," I tell her before pushing her against the wall behind a lunch cart that blocks us from view.

"What is he doing here?" Annette hisses.

"I don't know."

"Is he the same guy who grabbed us? I thought Lake said the Demon Dawgs captured them all?"

"He did. This guy must be another member."

We watch Joyce break off their intense conversation when Sylvia stalks up to her. The guy turns away from Sylvia and glances down the hall. Fisting his right hand, he punches his left before rubbing them together. I gasp when I recognize him from Francois' restaurant. He was part of the trio who threatened him.

"I recognize him," Annette whispers after he passes by without looking at us.

"You do? How?" I ask.

"From the video Pirate showed us. The way he pounds his fist into his hand. It's the same way the driver reacted when he saw you weren't in the car."

I study the man and realize she's right—the memory of that night when my car broke down. I recall seeing his reaction when he found I was no longer in my car. I share a glance with Annette before grabbing her hand and pulling her to the elevator. "We need to get downstairs and tell Levi. We have to follow him."

Levi sees us enter the lobby and rushes over when he sees our expressions. "What happened? What's wrong?"

We tell him what we saw.

Levi takes out his phone and calls Jack while he takes off his prospect kutte. We step outside to see the man walk quickly toward a white van parked nearby. He climbs into the passenger seat just before the driver reverses out of the parking spot.

Jack pulls up, and we all pile in.

"They're in that white van," Levi says.

Jack keeps cars between us and the van as we follow them. They don't try to lose us, so I'm hoping that means they haven't spotted the tail. When the van pulls to the side of the road behind a parked car, I wonder if they've caught on to us, but then I realize the situation is much worse. They leave the van wearing scrubs, surgical masks, and surgical caps. I glance toward the car to see a woman opening her car door.

Chapter Twenty-Seven: Lake

"What's his problem?" Toff asks me.

"Probably just worried about Coyote," I say, but I can't fight the nagging feeling that there is more to it than that. To say Coyote and Crow have a tumultuous relationship doesn't do it justice. Crow has always been jealous of Coyote and his position within the tribe. Growing up, I heard rumors that Crow had been in love with our mother before she married Dad. But no matter how often they clashed, Crow and Coyote always worked things out. Crow always has Coyote's back. "He probably feels like he failed Coyote by not being there when he needed him."

"I talked to the detective looking into the attack on Coyote," Toff says. "He doesn't have any leads, but he wanted to tell us that he'll release Coyote's house in the next few days. He has some of the paperwork bagged into evidence. I told him we might need access to it, depending upon what the lawyer needs for the petition."

I'm unsure how I feel about the cops having Coyote's documents. "Do you think we can trust them with those documents? They could make the paperwork disappear if they're susceptible to bribes."

Toff shrugs. "Nothing we can do about it. Hopefully, when I meet with the lawyer, she'll tell me she has everything she needs to proceed."

We're returning to New Orleans so Toff can meet with the lawyer who was working with Coyote and so I can help interrogate the assholes who kidnapped Annette and Olivia. Hex has kept them chilling in The Farm. I have little doubt that Abra and Dixie have softened them up. However, before we return to New Orleans, we plan to stop at the hospital to check on Coyote.

"How is he?" I ask Danny, who is sitting outside Coyote's room.

"Still unconscious."

"Anyone come by to see him?"

"A few people. One claimed to be your uncle. Colin spoke to him and turned him away. He wasn't happy about it. But we followed your orders. No one but the medical staff in or out." He nods at Colin, who hands him a cup of coffee from the cafeteria.

"Should we let your uncle in to see him?" Colin asks as he takes a sip of his coffee.

I considered allowing him access but decided against it. After all, he specifically said not to do him any favors. "No. Keep it staff only. Better that no one has access than to take any chances."

Toff eyes me but says nothing as we go into Coyote's room. The sight of him in the hospital bed still feels unreal.

"You don't trust Crow?"

"Honestly, I don't trust anyone but you and Annette. Do I think Crow attacked Coyote? No. But what if I'm wrong?"

"I don't think you're wrong keeping him out," Toff admits. "Honestly, Coyote and Crow have been arguing more and more lately. I don't know why, except that Coyote has been more secretive. Now I know why. The only thing they seem to agree upon these days is you."

"Me?"

"Becoming chief. Both want you to claim your legacy. They spent hours discussing how to convince you."

I shake my head. "What a waste of time. I have no intention of becoming chief."

Toff chuckles. "Remember, you are chief."

"Temporary," I growl.

Toff and I spend the next half hour talking to Coyote, hoping he'll hear us and wake up. Toff even tells him about my filling in as chief. We're interrupted by the same doctor who operated on Coyote.

"You're dad's doing better. His blood pressure is normal, and the wound is healing well. He isn't showing any signs of infection, which is good."

"Why hasn't he woken up yet?" Toff asks.

"He had a traumatic experience. His mind may be protecting him from facing the reality that someone tried to kill him."

Someone he knows and likely trusted, I silently add.

The ride to New Orleans gives me time to think. Zip and I follow Toff, who is in Annette's car. I'm excited to see Olivia again, even though we've only been apart for a few hours. In all my years, I've managed to maintain a calm presence on the outside while chaos swirls internally. However, Olivia calms the internal upheaval. I simply feel more in control when I'm with her.

At the clubhouse, we find Pirate sitting at the bar, drinking a beer. Zip ducks behind the bar and grabs three beers.

"Where is everyone?" I ask.

Pirate smirks. "Hex, Abra, and Dixie are out back. Cleo and Delphine went to look at potential restaurant sites with Nora."

"Where's Annette?" Toff asks.

"And Olivia?" I add, smacking Pirate on the back of the head. He knew who I was asking about. The fucker.

"Levi and Jack drove Annette and Olivia to the hospital," Pirate supplies. "Don't worry. They'll make sure nothing happens to either of them. Did you see the news?"

"No, why?"

"They found the body of Olivia's friend, Talia. I did some research and found that someone beat her death before tossing her into the river."

"Shit. How's Olivia holding up?"

"What do you think? She's pissed off. Went to the hospital to find out who isn't upset."

I shake my head at his comment. Whoever killed the woman will know to hide their disregard. "Can you guys show Toff where Annette's sleeping? I need to join Hex."

Pirate nods before I leave the clubhouse and point myself toward The Farm. The Farm was once a fishing shack sitting at the bayou's edge. It had been in disrepair when Hex repurposed it into our kill shack. Trees and shrubs surround the building, shielding it from view. Even though the lagoon it sits on is well-hidden from the main waterway. Anyone floating through the bayou would pass right by the inlet without knowing it's there. Hex tore down the wooden structure and replaced it with concrete blocks. The building is four times the size of the shack, so instead of just one room, The Farm boasts two cells, a bathroom with a shower, and a torture room.

Screams greet me when I open the door. Did I mention that The Farm is fully soundproof? Inside, I find a man hanging from a hook surrounded by Abra, Hex, and Dixie. He looks like a slab of meat in a butcher shop. The coppery smell of the blood dripping onto the floor adds to the ambiance. I assume the other two are either dead or back in the cells.

"You guys started without me?" I ask, just before Abra lands a punch to the guy's kidney.

"Just softening him up. Don't want you to have to waste time before getting your answers." Abra grabs the guy's hair and jerks his head so he's looking at me. One eye is bloodshot and sporting a bruise that will last longer than he will. "See, that guy? He's the chief of the tribe you've been hassling. Oh, and one of the women you kidnapped? Yeah, she belongs to him. If you're smart, and I've got fifty bucks that says you aren't, you'll answer every question he has before he takes out his knife and scalps you."

I smirk at Abra's speech. I've never considered scalping as a way to get info out of someone, but the look of terror in the bastard's eyes has me considering it. With the option in mind, I open the cupboard where Abra keeps his sharp instruments. Selecting an 8" knife with a bone handle, I move in front of him so he can see it. The blood drains from his face, making his bruises and cuts stand out more.

"Get that the fuck away from me," he whines as he tries to shake off Abra's hold.

"Let's start with something easy. Why the fuck did you assholes kidnap the women?"

I wave at Abra to release the guy's hair. He does so I can gather it in my fist. Placing the sharp edge of the blade against his skull, I press hard enough to create a line of blood that drips into his eyes. He screams and pisses himself.

"We were paid to grab them."

"Who fucking paid you?" I demand, digging the knife deeper.

"Someone from your tribe. He wanted us to create a diversion by kidnapping that guy you were with, but Wyatt wanted us to take the women. He had a buyer for them."

"Who's the buyer?" Hex demands.

"Don't know. Wyatt handles all that. He said they tried to grab the nurse once already, but she escaped."

So, whoever this Wyatt guy is, he's involved with the kidnappers.

"Where the fuck do we find Wyatt?" Hex demands.

"I don't know. He's working in New Orleans and moves around. Our job is to hassle the tribe."

"Why?" I ask.

"It's part of a plan. We're here to run the fucking filth out of our country. We're taking it back from the colored and reclaiming our birthright."

I snort. "My people were here before the white man came, asshole. Maybe we should be the ones cleaning the filth out. Let's start with the racist idiots like you."

"Fuck you!"

"No, fuck you," I say, slicing off a sliver of skin, complete with hair, and shoving it in his face as he screams. "Now, unless you want me to remove the rest of your scalp, you'll tell me everything."

Chapter Twenty-Eight: Olivia

I watch in horror as the young woman we saw taking the tour of obstetrics gets out of the car to greet the two men. When I move to open the door, Levi stops me.

"Hold on, let's see what happens."

"You know what's going to happen. They're going to kidnap that girl. We have to stop them."

"No, we need to follow them and figure out where they're hiding," Jack says.

"But…"

"Olivia, think about it. Even if we grab these two, we don't know how many more are out there. Besides, these two may lead us to your friend. We need to know where they're hiding," Levi explains.

"I know, but she's going to be so scared," I say as Annette clutches my hand.

We all watch as the men grab the woman, tie her up, and toss her into the back of the van. Annette's grip on my hand tightens. I feel so useless as I imagine how terrified the woman must be. Tears stream down my cheeks. When the van pulls away from the curb, Jack waits for them to turn the corner before pulling out to follow them.

About twenty minutes later, Jack pulls over as the white van pulls into a boarded-up mechanic's garage. The building has four bays and a reception area.

"This must be where they're hold up," Levi says. "Should we call

Hex?"

"Probably. Let me get out and look around. If I'm not back in ten minutes, call Hex. If they leave, follow them."

Jack hops out and races across the street. He ducks behind the abandoned building next door to the garage. We don't see him again until he returns to the driver's seat. "There are three men inside. I didn't see the girl. She might still be in the van." He takes out his phone and calls Hex.

He gives Hex a rundown of what we witnessed, ending the call after giving him our location.

"He's sending reinforcements. Once they get here, we'll drive the women back to the clubhouse."

"We aren't leaving," I tell Jack, ignoring the furious expression on Levi's face. "You need us here to help the woman. She's going to be terrified. Think a bunch of bikers will make her feel safe?"

"Olivia…" Levi starts, but Jack holds up his hand to stop him.

"Don't bother. It isn't our call. Let Hex and the others make the decision. For now, they're both safe in here. I'll watch the rear to ensure they don't sneak out the back."

"Why don't we just call the police?" Annette asks.

Levi and Jack have a conversation without words. Since they seem unwilling to answer, I take charge.

"We don't know if we can trust the police," I tell her. She frowns at me as I continue. "These guys are extorting money from several businesses in New Orleans. A woman who owned a bakery went to the cops and demanded they do something about the men. However, instead of arresting the men, the men kidnapped her and burned down her bakery. The cops said she burned the place down to collect the insurance. They ignored the eyewitness statement of someone who saw the men kidnap her and start the fire. If we call the cops, how do we know if the cops who come can be trusted?"

Jack gave me a quick nod before climbing out of the SUV and taking the path he had taken earlier.

We wait in silence. I'm staring at the building, wishing to see through the walls. When both passenger doors fly open, and two men slide in. Annette lets out a squeak while I jolt. However, the familiar scent of leather and wood calms me. Wrapping my arms around Lake, I relax into him. All my stress melts away knowing he's here.

"I take it Jack's watching the rear?" Hex asks from the front seat.

Levi nods. "He's been texting me. I let him know you're here.

What's the plan?"

"Why don't you drive the women back to the clubhouse, then come back."

"No," I say, leaning forward, only to have Lake pull me back against him.

"You'll both be safer at the clubhouse," Lake says. "Toff is there, too."

"We can help," I protest. "The woman they kidnapped will trust us before she trusts you. We can take care of her while you take care of the assholes who kidnapped her."

"She has a point," Hex says. "Cleo and Skylar were a great help when we rescued those kids."

"Okay, but you both stay in the SUV with Levi until we call for you," Lake demands.

"Of course."

When the guys don't get out, I turn a questioning look towards Lake. "It thought you guys were going in?"

Lake chuckles. "We are. We need to wait until it gets dark."

"They could be hurting her," I remind them.

"They aren't," Levi responds. "Jack's close enough to see and hear what's happening inside."

"Do you have a first aid kit in here?" Annette asks.

"Yeah," Lake says, reaching over the seat to lift the floor. Inside is a cavity filled with blankets and a duffle bag. He pulls the bag out and plops it on my lap.

"What else do you have back there?" I ask as Annette searches through the bag, and Lake hands me a blanket.

"You don't want to know," he replies.

"Okay, let's go," Hex says, opening his door. Lake kisses me before following his President.

It isn't completely dark outside. I can still see a sliver of light from the setting sun, but most of the area is in shadow. The guys quickly disappear from view. I brace myself for the sound of gunshots, but the night remains eerily quiet. With my eyes locked on the building, the sound of the car door opening has me jolting again. I glance at Levi, who is stepping out of the SUV.

"Let's go," he says as he opens my door.

"Go where?" Annette asks.

He gives us a questioning look. "I thought you two wanted to go inside to help the nurse they kidnapped?"

"Is it all over?" I ask in surprise. "I didn't hear anything."

"Were you expecting a war?" Levi asks with a smirk.

"Well, yeah. Maybe not a big one, but I expected to hear gunfire."

"They didn't need it. They caught the bastards unaware."

Annette and I climb out of the SUV. She's carrying the duffle bag with the supplies while I have the blanket.

"We're going to need more blankets," Levi says. "Hex said there are more victims."

Annette and I follow him to the rear of the SUV. He opens it and pulls out a stack of blankets. I spot a locked box tucked further back in the cavity. It doesn't take a genius to realize the box likely contains guns and ammo.

Levi takes the blankets and the duffle bag before leading us across the street. We step into the shop to hear the sound of male cussing and women weeping. Levi leads us through the empty lobby into the garage. There, we see three men zip-tied and kneeling on the floor. They're cussing at Abra, who stands over them. The prisoners threaten him and the rest of the club with everything from assassination to lynching. Abra ignores them. He focuses on his brothers as they lift two pregnant women out of the service pit.

Annette and I rush to wrap blankets around the two women shivering in the unheated garage. Pirate is helping the third woman, whom we spotted at the hospital, climb out of the pit.

"My name is Annette. I'm a doctor. This is Olivia. She's a nurse. Are you in any pain or have any injuries?"

"I'm Letitia," the oldest of the three women responds. "They didn't hurt us."

"But I wouldn't say no to some food and water," the second pregnant woman says. "My name is Jasmine."

"Levi, go grab some Gatorade and protein bars from the SUV. That will suffice until we can get you to a hospital," Hex says. "How long have you been here?"

"I've been here two days," Letitia says. "They brought Jasmine yesterday."

"Excuse me," the woman we saw kidnapped interrupts. "Why haven't the police and ambulance arrived yet? They should be here by now."

"They aren't coming," Hex tells her.

"Why not? You need to call them immediately."

"No cops," Hex says, causing her head to snap in his direction.

"What? Why not? They can't get away with this."

"They won't," Hex says.

She narrows her eyes at Hex, but we hear Jack shout out for help before she can respond. Jack calls for me in a voice strangled with emotion. I rush back into the waiting room and through a door into what used to be an office. Now, it's a makeshift bedroom with a mattress on the floor. Laying naked on the bed with blood covering her legs and face is a fourth woman. We don't need a rape kit to tell us what we already know. Those fuckers used this poor woman as their fuck toy.

"Oh my god," the woman next to me hisses.

Chapter Twenty-Nine: Olivia

The takedown was more straightforward than we expected. The three assholes inside didn't see us coming. When they realized we'd infiltrated the building, we already had them zip-tied and kneeling on the concrete floor.

The calls for help from the service pit have Jack searching for the controls. He raises the car so that it no longer blocks the space. When we have enough space, Pirate and I slide into the pit. We expect to find one woman; instead, we see three—two of whom are close to bringing two more people into the world. The woman we thought we were rescuing stands guard over the other two. She looks ready to fight us to the death.

Pirate and I lift our hands. "We aren't going to hurt you. We're here to rescue you. A friend of ours saw these assholes grab you and followed you here. They called us to come get you out. My name is Lake, and this is Pirate."

"Pirate?" she asks, her forehead creasing in confusion. "The same Pirate I spoke to yesterday about the Houma tribe?"

"You're Rey Montague? The attorney?"

"I am. What's going on? Why are you here?"

"Wait, you're the one who has been working with my father? Coyote?"

"Your father is Coyote?"

"Yes. My name is Lake. You have an appointment with my brother, Toff, tomorrow morning."

Rey lowers her defenses enough to let us help the other two women out of the pit. They introduce themselves as Letitia and Jasmine. Rey scrambles out of the pit once the other two women are topside. She helps them get comfortable while we wait for Levi to bring Annette and Olivia.

Rey paces while Annette and Olivia comfort the other two women. Hex sends Levi out to the SUV to grab them some nourishment. Abra stands guard over the three prisoners, but his eyes flash often to Rey. Her agitation is on full display.

"Excuse me," Rey says. "Why haven't the police and ambulance arrived yet? They should be here by now."

"They aren't coming," Hex tells her.

"Why not? You need to call them immediately."

"No cops," Hex says, causing her head to snap in his direction.

"What? Why not? They can't get away with this."

"They won't," Hex says.

A shout from Jack has us rushing through the waiting room and into what used to be an office. Inside, lying on a dirty mattress is a naked woman. Blood and bruises cover her body. The sight of the broken woman has Hex rushing back to our captives. Grabbing a fistful of hair, he yanks the first one up and knees him hard in his junk. The man screams out in pain before dropping to the floor. Hex kicks him several more times in the same spot before he passes out from the pain. Without breaking a sweat, he repeats the treatment on the other two men.

"What did you find?" Abra asks. We're all standing around the pieces of shit passed out on the floor.

"A woman. They brutalized her," Hex snaps out.

"Can we call the cops now?" Rey asks.

"Fuck the cops," Hex sneers. "Do you think the fucking cops are going to do anything about these mother-fuckers? They have the cops in their pockets, sweetheart."

"Not all of them. Not my brothers," Rey says, glaring at Hex. "My brothers will make sure they get what they deserve."

"You're brothers are cops?" I ask.

"Yes. I have three brothers, and they're all in the force. They're all good cops. One is in Boston, but the other two are here."

Hex studies her before responding.

"How about we compromise?" Hex says. "Levi and Jack will take all of you to the hospital. You can call your brothers from there and tell them what happened. Give them this address. Olivia and Annette can go with you. They can tell the cops how we found you."

"How can they explain?" Rey asks.

"Olivia and Annette saw you at the hospital just before spotting them," I tell her, nodding at the men. "We had a run-in with them before, so Jack followed them. They saw the men kidnap you, so they called us once they arrived here. These assholes tried to kidnap Olivia a few nights ago. She can tell her story to your brother."

"What about them?" Rey asks, nodding at the men.

"We want to talk to them. We'll hand them over to your brothers when they show up. Will that work?"

"You aren't going to kill them?"

"No. We may rough them up a bit, but we won't kill them. You have my word."

She glances at me. "Can I trust you to keep your word?"

I nod.

"Okay, I'll trust you."

"Thank you."

Levi backs the SUV into the garage so Jack can place the unconscious and broken woman into the back. He's lined the floor with blankets and covers her with another. I doubt she notices, but it's a nice gesture. Once everyone is loaded in, Hex stops Jack and Levi.

"Lose the kuttes. Ray may trust her brothers, but there's no sense leading them right to our doorstep. Levi, play the brother card to explain your reason for stepping in to help."

"Got it, Prez," Levi and Jack say together. They remove their kuttes and hand them over to Dixie to keep.

Once they're gone, we focus on our prisoners.

"Abra, if you'll do the honors," Hex says.

Abra finds a bucket and fills it with water. He dumps the bucket over the middle guy, whom we determined to be the leader. He sputters awake, his eyes narrowing on Hex.

"You fucking bastard. You're fucking dead." He lets out a groan of pain when he shifts to sit up. His complexion turns green as we all step back in case he spews.

Hex chuckles. "Big talk from a man with a broken dick."

"Just wait. Your fucking days are numbered spic." He spits toward Hex.

"You are fucking clueless, aren't you? I don't have time to give you a lesson in genetics or geography. You'll figure it out in prison. Why the fuck are you kidnapping women?"

"I'm not telling you shit."

Hex nods at Abra. With the quickness of a snake, Abra lashes out, slashing a deep groove from his eye to his mouth. Blood gushes from the wound as the no-longer cocky bastard screams.

"Unless you want him to match it on the other side, fucking talk. Why were you kidnapping women?"

"Money," he manages to say after spitting out blood.

"Someone paid you to kidnap women after disabling their cars?" Hex asks, getting a nod. "Who?"

"Don't know names. Two doctors."

"Where do you take them?"

Before he can answer, the asshole's phone rings, Abra reaches into the guy's pocket and pulls it out. He glances at the display. "Money Doc," he says. Then he holds the phone in front of the mangled face of our prisoner. I'm surprised when it unlocks the phone.

Abra hands it to Hex before yanking the prisoner's head back by his hair and placing the knife against his other cheek. The message is clear. Don't make a fucking sound, or he'll resemble Heath Ledger's Joker.

"Yo," Hex grunts into the phone. He listens for a minute before ending the call with "On it." He hands the phone to Pirate. "Seems like the doctor is ready for his delivery. Where?"

The man clamps his lips shut, so Abra digs the blade under his eye. His intentions are clear. Give up the address or give up the eye. It's his choice. Unsurprisingly, he rattles off an address.

Hex checks his watch and nods at Abra, who slams his gloved fist against the wound, knocking him out.

"Rey and the others should be at the hospital by now, so the cops will be here soon. Let's ride. We have a couple of doctors who are about to lose their licenses. Permanently."

Piling into the SUV, we take off with Zip driving.

"Shit, that was close," Zip says, looking in the rearview mirror. We all turn to see three cop cars pulling up to the garage. The lights flash and light up the building. No one is chasing us, so that's good.

The address the asshole gave us is for an abandoned restaurant. It sits on the river, surrounded by trees and an empty parking lot.

"I know this place," Abra says. "I've eaten here before. They had seating on two floors and the back deck."

We park on the road, out of sight of the building. Under the cover of the trees, we surround the place. The building has a Victorian look, complete with window shutters. Whoever was inside closed the shutters, but we could still see the light filtering through. The shutters work in our favor because we can approach the building without anyone inside seeing us.

Zip and I cover the sides while Dixie and Pirate cover the front. Hex and Abra are at the back, where Abra works to open the lock. The front door opens as we get Hex's text letting us know they're in. Two men in suits step out. Another pair of men follow them, wearing cargo pants and carrying military-grade weapons.

"They should be here soon," the suit says. "Three women. Two are ready to pop. They won't be a problem. The third is only four months along. Get them all inside and strapped down. Carver can check them out then."

Dixie sends a text letting Hex and Abra know what's happening outside. Hex replies with an order to take them out. The four of us converge on the men. Zip and I take out the muscle by slitting their throats. We let them drop to the ground just as Dixie and Pirate have the two suits face dirt in the mud with their wrists zip-tied behind their backs.

Hex steps out of the front door. With a clenched jaw, he glowers at the men in suits. "You two fucked up," he snarls at them before glancing at Zip and me. "Dump those bodies in the river, then come inside. Better prepare yourself."

Zip and I silently lug the bodies to the rear of the building and dump them into the river. They'll either float downstream and get found or become alligator food. I realize this is close to where they fished out the body of Olivia's friend.

"Not sure I want to see what's inside," Zip says as we return to the restaurant. Neither of us are prepared for what we find inside.

Chapter Thirty: Olivia

We make the drive mostly in silence, except for the occasional heart-breaking whimper from the broken woman lying on the floor of the SUV. Jack pulls up to the Emergency entrance of Tulane Hospital. I rush inside to get help.

"We need a gurney and two wheelchairs," I order the nurse covering the desk. "We have three victims. One is a possible rape victim. The other two are kidnap victims, and both are pregnant."

The next few minutes are chaotic as nurses and orderlies rush outside to help the victims.

"I'm going to offer my help. The women may feel more comfortable with me there," Annette says before following the two pregnant women.

"We need to call the police," the head nurse tells me.

Rey steps in. "The police will be here shortly."

The nurse nods and rushes off.

"Have you called your brother then?" I ask, knowing that Hex and the others don't have much time if he's on his way.

"Not yet. I promised your friends time. I'll give it to them. But first, I want to know what you know."

I explain how I worked with Dr. Marcia Carver and Talia Bonaparte at Omega Hospital before they transferred to Tulane and disappeared. Rather than explain how the Demon Dawgs determined the tampering of the cars connected to their disappearances, I fast-forward to my attempted kidnapping. I describe how someone stole my phone and tampered with my car.

"The patient I had told me a story of how her car broke down before two men in a white van tried to grab her. A stranger stepped in and stopped them. When my car broke down, I remembered her story. Getting out of the car, I hid. That was the right move since those guys who grabbed you showed up shortly after. I watched them search for me."

"Talia Bonaparte? Isn't that the girl whose body they just found?"

"Yes. I heard they found their cars abandoned on the side of the road. Like mine had been."

"And mine. I just had my car into service a few days ago. I shouldn't have had any trouble. You think they tampered with my car?"

"I do. Hex and the others think that's how they were able to kidnap the women. They found themselves stranded and easy prey to two men dressed like doctors on the way home from the hospital. The scrubs and the masks hid them, but not in a way that made the women consider the men were hiding their identities. Talia and Marcia likely thought someone from work saw them and stopped to help."

Rey nods. "That's what I thought. I'd just been at the hospital to get a tour of the facility. A nice nurse showed me around and answered all my questions. I saw several of the staff wearing similar scrubs. Some wore masks. When I saw both men exit the van, I wasn't concerned. I didn't realize my mistake until it was too late."

"I know."

You saw them kidnap me?" Rey asks.

"We did. I'm sorry we didn't step in sooner. We followed the van and didn't realize the men targeted you until it was too late."

"Why were you following them?"

"Annette and I saw one here, and we recognized him. We told Levi and Jack, who followed them."

"Considering what we found, I'm glad you didn't interfere. Those women would be in worse shape if you'd stopped them instead of following them. The person in charge, Hex? He stressed that he didn't trust the cops. Is that just because he's a biker?"

I shake my head. "No. Those men weren't just kidnapping women. They were extorting money from businesses. One victim owns a restaurant, Francois. He told us what happened to a woman who refused to pay their fee and reported them to the police. The assholes burned down her bakery. Francois saw them do it, and he saw them

kidnap the owner. I think she might be the one we found in the office."
I don't know if this is true, but unfortunately, it feels right. "When
Francois reported what he saw to the cops, the assholes showed up at
his restaurant and beat him before raising their fee. They told him to
mind his own business."

"Shit. I hate dirty cops. Okay, I'll call my brother and tell him what's
going on." She checks her watch. "It's been forty-five minutes. Do you
think that's long enough?"

I shrug. "I think so. Doubt it will take Hex and others long to get the
information they need."

Rey takes out her phone and makes the call. "Max. It's Rey. I need
your help." Rey gives him a quick summary of the evening's events. I
smirked as the voice on the other end rose in volume as she spoke.
"I'm at the Tulane Hospital with the victims and four of the people
who rescued us. You'll find the men who kidnapped me tied up inside
an abandoned garage. Look, there is a strong possibility that these
guys own a few cops. You need to make sure you trust whoever you
send." Rey gives him the address before ending the call.

"Max is sending patrol officers to the garage. He promised only to
send those he knows he can trust, along with our brother, who is also a
detective. These guys won't get away with it."

I don't respond. Hex is giving the cops a chance to clean up this
mess, and I know he'll take care of the kidnappers if they fail.

While we wait for her brother, we watch two men rush into the
hospital. They're frantic as they ask about their pregnant wives.

I move toward them. "You're married to Letitia and Jasmine?"

"Yes," both men respond together.

"They are both with a doctor now. They took them up to obstetrics
to check on the babies. You can head up there. There is a nurse on staff,
Sylvia. Let her know that Olivia sent you up. The cops are on their way
and will need to speak to them."

The two men rush to the elevator while I return to Rey. We barely
have time to take seats before another man rushes in. He has Rey's
bronze-colored hair and green eyes. However, he's also a foot taller
with broad shoulders—the material of his suit strains against his arm
muscles. Rey disappears in his embrace.

"Thank god you're okay," he mutters.

"Thanks to Olivia and her friends," Rey responds before pulling
away. "Olivia, this is my brother Maxwell. Max. Max, this is Olivia."

He motions for me to take a seat across from him. Rey sits next to me while he takes out his notebook. "Okay, hit me."

I give him my story, leaving out the Demon Dawgs. If Rey wants to rat them out, then she can, but I'm not volunteering any information. He raises an eyebrow but says nothing when I mention Talia going missing and how I thought her disappearance connected to Dr. Carver's.

"You know we found Ms. Bonaparte's body in the river?"

I nod before continuing with my story. The detective stops me when I mention my car breaking down and losing my phone.

"You were here at the hospital when you lost your phone?"

"I didn't lose it. I think someone took it and dumped it in the hamper since I never went near it. I never use it. Someone came in while I was taking a shower and took my phone. I think it was the same person who took my keys and sabotaged my car."

"You're certain it was sabotage?"

"Yes. My boyfriend had someone check it out, and I saw the feed showing a man doing something under the hood of my car."

His head snaps up. "You saw him? Did you get a good look at him?"

"No, because he wore a skull cap and a surgical mask. He was also wearing scrubs. Just like the men who later pulled up behind my broken-down car and who kidnapped Rey."

"So, you don't know who sabotaged your car and who kidnapped Rey?"

"No. I know. Now. I recognized the mannerisms of the man who tried to kidnap me. After he realized I wasn't in the car, he punched his right hand into his left. He did the same thing when I saw him at Francois' and earlier today when I saw him here in the hospital."

"Wait, what?"

I continue with my story and tell him everything about running into the men at the restaurant, the extortion they're running, and how we came to be following them when they kidnapped Rey. Detective Montague doesn't interrupt me again. "You might want to talk to the nurse he was meeting here. Her name is Joyce Eloise. I told her about almost being kidnapped and asked her to warn the staff. She didn't."

"Okay, how did you overpower the three men we found at the garage?"

"Oh, well, that wasn't me. My brother and his friend were with us. We called in my boyfriend and his friends to help since we didn't know how many men were inside the garage."

"You didn't think to call the cops for help?"

I look at him until we make eye contact. "No. Because I know these men have cops in their pockets." He gives me a disbelieving look until I tell him about the extortion and how the cops didn't believe or chose not to help the victims.

Before he can ask me further questions, my phone rings. Lake's name shows on the display.

"Olivia? Are you still with Rey?"

"Yes. I'm talking to her brother right now."

"The detective? Good. We need him to come right away. We found the rest of the missing women."

Chapter Thirty-One: Lake

We were not prepared.

Not prepared for the smell of unwashed bodies and human waste.

Not prepared for the sight of almost two dozen pregnant women strapped to beds.

Not prepared for the sounds of weeping and the prevailing cloud of despair that permeated every inch of the room.

"Where the fuck is she?" Screams a woman, pounding on our prisoner. "You mother-fucking bastard. What did you do to her?"

Hex grabs her, wrapping his arms around her even as she struggles to escape. He's whispering, but I don't think she's listening. I recognize her from her picture. Dr. Marcia Carver. Olivia's friend.

While Zip moves to help Pirate and Dixie free the women, I go to help Hex. "You're Dr. Carver?" I ask her.

She stills, but Hex doesn't release his grip. Probably seeing the hate-filled glare she sends at the man she attacked. "Do I know you?"

"No. But I'm a friend of Olivia Delacroix. She's why we've been looking for you and Talia."

"Talia's dead," Marcia says, nodding at the men. "Those fucking bastards let their hired thugs beat her to death right in front of us. We had to watch as they destroyed her."

Abra yanks the man Marcia attacked up off the ground and punches him hard in the liver. I wince when I see he's wearing his brass knuckles. Getting hit in the liver hurts like a bitch. The pain sucks all the oxygen out of the man's lungs. He can't manage a scream. Abra repeats the punishment on the second asshole.

"Who are they?" Hex asks.

"Dr. Anton Calder and Dr. John Merkel," Marcia spits.

"You're fucking doctors?" Hex snarls. "What the fuck is wrong with you?"

"They're not doctors. They're fucking monsters. This asshole stole my baby." Marcia breaks loose to kick at Dr. Calder.

"That's not how you get him to talk, sweetheart. Hit him where it hurts," Abra says, taking off his brass knuckles and handing them to her. She stares at them before looking between Abra and the man at her feet.

A look of demonic pleasure crosses over her pretty features as she slides them on. She pulls her arm back and slams the mental prongs into Calder's junk. I wince at the sight but can't hold back the chuckle when his high-pitched scream echoes around the room. The other women cheer her on.

"Tell me where my baby is," Marcia screams at the man who whimpers in pain.

Abra shakes him. "Tell her, or I'll deliver a kick that will send your pathetic cock into your stomach."

"Okay," he wheezes out. "I gave him to a man who promised to take the baby out of the country. I couldn't let them trace the kid back to me."

Marcia collapses against Hex, who wraps his arm around her to steady her.

"Give us a name," Hex orders.

"Mikel, something. I don't know who he is. He worked for one of our clients."

"Nero?" Hex asks.

The guy jerks at the mention of Hex's dead father-in-law.

"When was the baby born?" I ask Marcia.

She shares the date, and I look at Hex. Could it be? The timing was right. So was the player, Mikel. He brought two babies and several other children onboard a ship setting sail for South America. All were destined for grim futures until the Demon Dawgs intervened and rescued the children. We returned all the children to their families except for the two babies.

"Any chance these assholes gave Mikel two babies?" Hex asked her.

She nods. "Yes. A second baby was born only a few hours after mine. His." Marcia nods at Merkel, who has tried to make himself disappear. He goes green when we all turn to look at him. "Some poor girl that he impregnated and brought here. She didn't survive the birth."

"I don't want to get your hopes up, but we found two babies on a cruise ship around that time. The man who brought the babies on board was Mikel," Hex explains. "I don't know if either of those babies is yours, but we'll find out."

"Really?" Marcia looks at Hex with heartbreaking hope.

"Lake, call Olivia. See if she's still with Rey. We need ambulances and the cops to take over. Marcia, can you go with Lake?"

She nods and lets me take her arm. I lead her to a bed next to a woman who looks ready to give birth at any second—Hex kneels to talk to the two doctors. I don't know what he's saying, but the fear on their faces tells me he's making a point.

Olivia answers on the second ring. After learning she's still at the hospital and talking with Rey's brother, I give her our location and tell her to send the detective and every ambulance they have.

Hex finishes with the prisoners and comes to join us. "Olivia was still with Rey and Rey's brother. They're on their way here now. What are we going to do with them? Are we taking them back to the clubhouse?"

"No. Too risky. Besides, we don't need anything from those two assholes."

"Except for them to die after what they did to these women," Pirate argues.

"They'll get theirs. All we would do is kill them after inflicting some pain. Let them rot in some prison cell. My guess is they'll get their asses beat daily by the prisoners once they learn these assholes were selling infants."

"What if they get off?" Zip asks. "Two rich white guys? Odds are in their favor."

"I already told them what we'd do to them if they didn't confess."

"Thank you," Marcia says. "Thank you for finding us. Some of these women have been prisoners for almost a year. First as sex slaves, then once they got pregnant, those assholes had us caring for them so they could sell the babies."

"I'm guessing they took you and Talia to care for the women?"

"Talia, yes, but they grabbed me because I was pregnant with Calder's child. He and I worked together at Omega Hospital. He pursued me for weeks, but I resisted until he wore me down. Of course, once he had me, he moved on. Bastard. I can't believe I was such a fool."

"This isn't on you. This is on him," I assure her.

"Maybe. But I knew better. I knew Calder's reputation. We lasted six weeks before he dumped me for a nurse who had just transferred to Omega from a hospital out of state. I transferred to Tulane Hospital when I realized I was pregnant. I debated telling him but figured he'd find out, so I did the mature thing. I met him for coffee and told him the news. He freaked out. Then, a few days later, he called and asked to meet. He told me he had time to come to terms with becoming a father and wanted to discuss the future. He came over for dinner. I woke up locked in a room and chained to the bed. That's when the horror started."

"Did he try to abort the baby?" I ask.

"Surprisingly, no. I almost wish that was what he'd done. Instead, he told me he owned me and that I would never be free again. He took me out of the room and into hell. Women were chained to beds while men paid to rape them. Calder and Merkel told me to care for the women, or they'd tie me to a bed. They forced me to treat those poor girls. At first, I refused, so they grabbed the nearest girl and slit her throat. The next day, they had a new girl chained to that bed. She was young and still a virgin. I don't think she was older than sixteen. They told me I could either care for the girls they had or they'd dispose of the girls and grab new ones. I treated the women. I hated myself but didn't want them to break another girl."

"You said you were in a building. So, not this building?" Hex asks.

"No, I think it used to be an office building. There were multiple floors. Not sure how long we were there. Long enough to have my baby and lose him. Maybe a week or two after that, some kid showed up and told Merkel that they were about to get invaded by bikers."

"What did this kid look like?"

"Young. Maybe nineteen. He had on a vest with the word Prospect on the back." The rest of her description told us all we needed to know. Fucking Irish had warned the bastards. That's how they knew we were coming and why they cleared out the night we attacked.

"They killed those women," Marcia murmurs. "All of them. They walked around and slit their throats. The fuckers said it was a shame to waste them but that they could replace them. The only women they didn't kill were the ones who were pregnant. He brought us here."

Hex stalks over to the prisoners and yanks Merkel up by his tie. "Do you have another fucking whorehouse?"

Merkel sneers at Hex until Hex hauls back and punches him twice in the liver and then in the throat. Dropping Merkel back to the ground, Hex stomps hard on the man's left hand and then his right before smashing his kneecaps. As Merkel curls up into a fetal position, Hex turns his attention to Calder. "Want the same? Or are you going answer the fucking question?"

"No, we don't. I swear it. We haven't had time to set it up yet."

A disturbance at the door draws our attention. "Police!" shouts the cops as they stream into the building. Calder looks relieved until they slap on the cuffs.

Chapter Thirty-Two: Olivia

As I helped the last woman into the waiting ambulance, I finally let the tears fall for them. Some were already pregnant when those assholes grabbed them off the street, but several became pregnant from rape. I watch the cops lead Drs. Calder and Merkel away in handcuffs, but part of me wishes the guys had killed them.

Lake steps up behind me, and I lean into his embrace.

"Are you okay?" he asks.

"No, not really. I can't believe what those poor women went through. They're lucky you found them." I look around for cops before continuing. "Why didn't you just kill them?"

Lake chuckles before kissing the top of my head. "Can't say we didn't consider it. They forced Marcia to deliver more than one baby. Those assholes have the answers. They won't find jail a pleasant experience."

"Will they go to prison? Our court system doesn't often prosecute white men, wealthy white men. They can barter their freedom for the location of those babies."

"If that happens, then we'll deliver our form of justice," he promises me.

"Good," I say, turning to snuggle into his chest. I just get comfortable when his phone rings.

"Yeah," he says. He still has one arm around me, so I feel it when he stiffens. I shift to look up at his face. "When? Has he said who attacked him? Why the hell is he waiting? Okay, that's fine. I'm on my way."

"Was that about your dad?"

"Coyote woke up. I need to call Toff and get to the hospital."

"I want to go with you," I tell him.

He leans his head against mine. "Thank god because I need you with me. Could you do me a favor and tell Rey that Toff will call her later?" He checks his watch. "They planned on meeting at eight, which is only a few hours away. I need to tell Hex that we're taking off."

While Lake goes to tell Hex, I search for Rey and find her talking with her brother.

"This is fucking bizarre," Rey says when I reach her. "This is where they would have taken me. I don't think I can ever repay you for rescuing me."

"Same," Detective Montague says, smiling at me as he pulls his sister close.

"Does that mean we can go?" I ask the detective. "Lake got a call from the hospital. Coyote woke up and asked to see him and Toff. Lake's reaching out to Toff and expects he'll be going, too. He'll need to postpone his meeting with you."

"That's okay. I have other cases that I'm working on. Have Toff call me, and we'll set up a meeting. Maybe I can visit the hospital later and talk with them."

"I might have more questions for you and the club. Yes, I know who they are—the Demon Dawgs. I've seen them around town. We have to keep an eye out for those who could cause problems. However, in this case, they did good."

I smile my thanks. "I'll let them know you will reach out. They're good men. All of them."

Returning to Lake, he helps me get into the SUV. "Detective Montague wants to talk to you later. He said he'll have more questions. He also knows you're the Demon Dawgs."

Hex, who is sitting in the front seat, nods. "I thought he might."

I expect the guys to stop at the clubhouse, but Jack keeps driving. "Are they coming with us?" I ask Lake. "What about Toff?"

"Toff will meet us there. He went to pick up Annette."

Lake says nothing more about why Hex and the others are coming with us, but I can figure it out. Once he gives them a name, the club will help Lake track down Coyote's attacker.

We enter the lobby, where Lake and I break off to take the elevator to Coyote's floor. When we exit the elevator, Lake takes off at a run. I'm confused until I see Colin lying on the floor outside Coyote's room. I drop down beside him while Lake shoves into Coyote's room. I hear scuffling and consider running downstairs to get Hex and the others, but the elevator door opens, and Toff steps out.

"Lake's in Coyote's room; help him," I shout at Toff, who rushes inside while Annette drops across from me.

"Someone knocked him out," I say unnecessarily, considering the blood on the back of his skull.

"Where is everyone?" Annette asks, just as a doctor and nurse turn the corner. They come over to help, letting me check on Lake and his family.

Inside Coyote's room, I find Colin's brother, Danny, unconscious on the floor. Stepping outside, I tell the doctor that he has another patient. Annette leaves Colin in their hands and joins us.

Lake shoves Crow against the wall, his hand behind his back. Toff pulls a thick zip tie from Lake's pocket and hands it to him.

Lake fastens Crow's wrists behind his back before shoving him to the floor.

"Why the hell were you trying to kill Coyote?" Lake demands. "Are you the one who stabbed him?"

"Yes," Coyote responds. "That's why I asked for you to come. I didn't want to call the police. He's still my brother."

"Why did you want to kill Coyote?" Lake repeats his question to Crow.

"Because he deserves to die. He's taken everything from me. He has gotten everything he wants all my life, and I have gotten nothing. Now he's trying to steal my money."

"What money?" Coyote asks.

"The money I would get for selling land to the oil company. I've been buying up abandoned properties throughout our territory. But you would ruin everything if you got the government to recognize our tribe. The land wouldn't be mine to sell. It would belong to the fucking tribe."

"You betrayed our tribe over money?" Coyote asks with disgust.

"Why the fuck not? What has the tribe ever done for me? What have you ever done for me? Except take everything that mattered? You stole the woman I loved and claimed our son as your own."

Lake shakes his head. "What are you talking about? How did he steal the woman you loved? Do you mean Mom?"

"She was mine first!" Crow screams. "We would have been happy together, but he stole her! But I had my revenge. I had her before you did. She was mine, if only for a few hours. Long enough to make sure she was pregnant with my son!"

"You raped her?" Coyote yells out. "You mother-fucker. I'll kill you. She didn't love you, she loved me!"

"She had my son. My son will be chief, and I'll have control of the tribe!"

Lake's head snaps back as if someone punched him. "What did you say?"

"You're my son. Lenora and I had a night of passion before she married Coyote. She loved me but had to marry him. Nine months later, she had you. You are my son. Not his."

"You bastard! She didn't love you. She liked you, but she didn't love you. She loved me. You destroyed her. She never got over what you did to her."

"You raped my mother?" Lake asks, his voice is soft and lethal.

"No! Of course not. She wanted me, but she couldn't risk anyone finding out. I had to persuade her to give in to us."

Lake rushes forward and punches Crow in the face. "Persuade her? You fucking persuaded her? Persuasion isn't consent. You bastard."

"No, no, it wasn't like that. I swear. Lenora loved me."

I leave Annette to tend to Danny and go to Lake. He trembles as I wrap my arms around his waist and give him my strength. The door opens to let in two security guards. They take Crow out, who continues to scream about being the man Lenora loved and losing it all to his older brother.

"Lake...," Coyote calls out, causing Lake to tighten his hold on me. "Lake, look at me. I'm your father. I raised you. It doesn't matter what happened. You are my son."

"But, there are doubts?" Lake asks, looking at Coyote.

Coyote opens and closes his mouth several times before speaking. "Yes. There were doubts, but I swore to Lenora that I would never treat you differently. It's why I want you to become chief. Because as my oldest, it is your legacy."

Lake lets out a dark chuckle. "I never wanted to be chief."

"I know, but I couldn't betray my oath to your mother. You are my son."

"I am your son. Biology doesn't matter. Being chief doesn't matter. I love you, Dad. I always have, and I always will. But you must get over the expectation that I will claim my legacy. My sperm donor doesn't change the fact that Toff is your successor. We've wasted years arguing about this, and now there is a real possibility that Toff is your firstborn son instead of me. But you know what? That doesn't matter. Not really. Make Toff your successor. Mom would understand, and you'll do what's best for you, Toff, the tribe, and me."

Coyote studies his two sons for several long seconds before he nods in agreement. "You're right. I let my promise to your mother blind me. I don't think she cared if you became chief; she just wanted to ensure I didn't treat you differently."

When my phone rings, I take it out to see Rey's number.

"Hello, Rey. Are you looking for Toff?" I answer, putting the call on speaker.

"No, I'm looking for Lucifer's Heir. Tell him to give me back what's mine, or his assistant will pay the price."

"But, I don't know anyone…" I start, but the line goes dead. I look at Lake.

"We need to find Abra," Lake says, leaving the hospital room.

Author's Thank You

Thank you so much for reading Lake's Legacy. I apologize for the delay in its release. Writing this book has been a struggle for me because I faced many challenges in my personal life. My dog, Luna, went completely blind and had trouble walking. The previous year, she had been diagnosed with low thyroid levels and began experiencing heart issues. I knew we were likely going to lose her, which broke my heart. We ended the year in the worst possible way. Our last cat, Shadow, decided she was finished, and we had to euthanize her the day after Christmas. Then, on December 31st, we had to put Luna to sleep. So, I'm feeling a bit overwhelmed at the moment.

If you have any comments or see any issues, please email kara@karalanebarstow.com or visit my website at https://klbarstow.com/. Nothing draws me out of a book I'm reading faster than a mistake, so I've done multiple edits. However, if I missed anything, I'd appreciate a note so I can fix it.

You can connect with me via Facebook https://www.facebook.com/KLBarstow or search for KL Barstow and Twitter @BarstowKara.

If you enjoyed the book, I would greatly appreciate it if you could consider leaving a review. When searching for my next read, I depend on others' reviews to help inform my choices. Reviews assist me as an author and help readers like you discover books they might enjoy. I hope you appreciate my writing style and the story enough to recommend it.

Abra's Acquisition, Book Four of Demon Dawgs New Orleans, comes out November 2025.

Made in United States
North Haven, CT
07 March 2025

66567570R00089